The Trail Planet With Hammocks

Chapter 1

B rain Nugget

AROUND 3:00 IN THE morning May 7th 2004 I was gently awoken. A faint aroma of gardenia blossom in the air. Of itself odd. I had lit no candles or burnt any incense. A ghostly, misty image of a hippie, granola, backpacker looking guy was at the end of my bed. A little scary but he seemed sort of mellow. I was thinking, 'It's a dream anyway; Nothing to worry.'

Ghost hippie said, "I'm not a ghost. I'm a hologram."

This helped me understand what was happening. Earlier that day I'd read a long article about several people who claimed to have been visited by holograms that spoke to them. These stories were outnumbering alien abduction stories lately. Really cool dream for me.

"This is not a dream Sparky. A nugget has been implanted in your brain and the nugget transmits this image of me into your room. I cannot interact with you. I only have user information for you. There is a 5 millimeter sphere implanted in your brain.

This sphere, technical name, brain nugget, will transmit to and receive from a brain nugget implanted in a woman named Wanda. When you sleep you will see, hear, taste, smell and experience whatever she touches. You will be able to communicate. Wanda is a humanoid from The Trail Planet With Hammocks, formerly known as Gweebon. You will have a little soreness just left of midpoint at the base of the back of your skull. Do not worry. This time tomorrow you will hardly

1

notice. It will only hurt if you bump the area or rub it or brush it too hard. It is very important that you do not have the brain nugget removed. If so, you will die. It has been cloaked to appear as normal tissue if observed from any current imaging technology on the Earth. It contains no metals so if an MRI is performed it will not be sucked out of your head.

You won't hear her thoughts, but you will hear her when she speaks. When you want to communicate with her, you can open a channel for her to hear your thoughts. To open the channel you have to think the word, Satchmo. To close the channel, think the word, Harpo. As previously stated, when she speaks you will hear her. Hammockers speak English, because it is the universal spoken and written language."

You have been chosen for this honor. You have no choice but to experience this. If you die, of course, Wanda will no longer receive from you. The brilliant scientists at The Trail Planet With Hammocks Bio-Com Research Institute have observed you for a year and are confident you will benefit.

Ghost Hippie stopped talking, just floated at the end of my bed.

If this was not a dream I would have many questions. But even if this was real, Ghost Hippie is just a projected image with sound. He can't answer questions. If this were real, I might be getting angry. Maybe I don't want to have a brain nugget from this Trail Planet in my head. Maybe I would have preferred a choice in the matter.

I touched my neck just left of center at the base of my skull and it was tender and slightly welted.

Ghost Hippie faded away.

About 3:30 in the morning now. Really need to sleep. Have to be at work at Stupentious Financial at 8:00 where I hold a position titled Mediocre Systems Analyst in the IT department. Got my start as a logician in the Cobol language. Mostly now I gather and report data as needed by the people in various departments in the company and I attend meetings where we try to figure out what the latest regulations are really requiring. It's more art than science. Mostly I try to maintain a balance of the joy experienced interacting with my close work associates and the gnawing discomfort I feel in my internal organs thinking in the manner required for the tasks I'm paid to do.

But, how can I go to sleep. I'm already asleep.

May as well make coffee. According to the old saying, if I can smell the coffee I must be awake.

I do, I can smell the coffee. My knee aches in the normal morning fashion. Much sinus drainage as usual when waking. Eyesight blurry. Check. I am indeed awake. Touched the back of my neck. Yep, still tender.

On my deck by my pool I enjoy my coffee and a cigarette. I'm in the process of quitting. Right now this coffee and cigarette are really pleasant on this mercifully cool and astounding low humidity morning in Mississippi in the deep southeast of the USA.

This sore spot on my neck is most curious. I'd go to sleep now if I could, but I can't. No way.

Chapter 2

Take a Break

THE TRAIL PLANET WITH HAMMOCKS

On my way to Stupentious, some guy thought I shouldn't have gone ahead of him in the roundabout. He drove a macho, big engined, extra cab pickup and was towing a twenty foot bay fishing boat. I slipped in just before him. He floored his truck, trying to take the inside track round the roundabout. Adrenalin shot through my system. He was about an inch from making contact with my little pickup. I'd've moved over to the right but deep wholes in the concrete were there and a small barrier. I goosed my truck and shot out of the roundabout just ahead of him. I held up my cell phone so he could see I was dialing. Wanted him to think I was calling the police. Leaning down I pretended to pull something from under my seat and place it on the seat beside me. Guess it worked. When we reached the four-lane he passed me in a civilized manner. No glares. No obscene gestures.

Still coming down from the adrenalin charge, I think, 'Last night I have a Brain Nugget stuck in my brain by some institute on a planet called The Trail Planet With

Hammocks, and this morning I'm nearly crashed into by a disturbed, fragile, psychotic nitwit. Thank God it's Friday and I had already arranged for next week off to go to the Gulf Shores Alabama area.'

I called my boss and asked if I could add today to my vacation. He said yes.

My workmates can easily handle my tasks for the next six work days. Most can be put off a week anyway. My assignments were important but not crucial. Such is the life of a

Senior Mediocre Systems Analyst.

Filling my extra large go-cup to the rim before leaving for work seemed especially fortuitous this day. Good coffee and good cheap cigarettes for my drive to the Super Blaster Drive-in. The Super Blaster, as you know, spreads the word in their marketing that they will not bow down to the demands of the elites who promote nanny-state policies concerning food. The Super Blaster International Mega Quick Copious

Foods Corporation sells Mega Meals, Super Mega Meals and Super Blaster Mega Copious Meals. This fine morning I have a hankering for Super Mega Texas Toast Breakfast Sandwich Meal. I ordered the bacon, egg and cheese variety. My choice of tots is spicy Mexican. My choice of drink is the real cola loaded with real sugar. All are Super Mega sized of course. Gave the car-hop a nice three dollar tip and an innocent congenial smile.

Made it home, peed, sang the Super Mega Foods jingle, warmed up my Super Mega foods, served up a big glob of ketchup for my tots, sat on the couch, turned on the TV and ate. Watched a Science channel show about Black Holes that I'd seen before. I like Black Holes so I didn't mind watching again.

Feeling a little strange. Is it the Brain Nugget or just the usual strange? I couldn't say.Just the normal strange. I think. This Super Mega Bacon Egg and Cheese Toaster is good.I dab my Mexican Tater Tots in the ketchup. Slurping my Cola. This is good. This is good eating. They say a black hole the size of a bowling ball has the mass of three thousand suns. Or did they say thirty million? Either way that's really something. They're pretty sure that the level of gravitational force associated with an object is proportionately greater the greater the mass of the object. So those puppies have a lot of gravitational pull.

Gravity is so weird. It attracts everything; anything with mass that is. Mushing my Tater Tots with my fork I convert them to Hash Browns and blend them with my ketchup glob and add more ketchup on top.

Some good Toaster and Tots and thinking about black holes and gravity. Getting very sleepy now. What if what Ghost Hippie said is all true?

Chapter 3

I Nod Off

"Sparky, hey Sparky. How you feeling? Remember you have to think the word Satchmo for me to hear your thoughts."

I thought, 'Think Satchmo? Really?'

"Yes, really, that's it. I can hear you thinking now."

"I'm Wanda, your Brain-Nugget partner. See my hands? You should be able to see what I see."

'I do,' I thought. 'Your hands are tanned and I like the silver ring with the small green stone.'

"Yeah, hey, me too. A good friend gave it to me."

"Can you see the beach and feel this wind?"

I thought, 'I can. It's beautiful there. This feels good. I love the light sand and the blue-green ocean, always have.'

"That's good. I was asleep when you were eating the Super Mega meal, so I could see you were eating a carby, fatty meal. I expected you'd be napping soon. Somehow I woke myself up to greet you. Welcome to The Trail Planet With Hammocks. You will love it here, I'm pretty sure. I'm curious about Earth too. This should be fun.

I enjoyed your flexing in the mirror and your rousing rendition of the Super Mega Foods jingle."

Wanda sang.

Super Mega Foods is super mega freedom

Super Mega Foods is super mega freedom

Super Mega Foods is super mega freedom

Super duper mega copious

I thought, 'It feels good being in a healthy body energetic. You must be in good shape.'

"Yeah, I guess so, compared to you."

'I've put on a few pounds of fat. It's true.' I thought.

She said, "I can't explain everything to you about all this. I'm just supposed to show you around. I'm going into the water."

'Kind of cold,' I thought. 'Are there sharks here?'

"I don't think so."

This feels great. There are fish jumping nearby. Refreshing, wooh, I felt an unfamiliar tingle when her breasts hit the cool water. Wanda swims like a pro. We swam further from the beach than I would have. I say we because it feels like it's me. Me if I was in great shape and I inhabited a female body. Pinkish, blue iridescent, six inch fish jump near as we swim. This makes me a little uneasy. On Earth where the baitfish are so are the predators. We're about 300 yards from the beach. Swimming out here like a seal.

I think, 'If Wanda gets devoured by a shark I'll feel the pain but I won't die, unless I have a heart attack. If she's eaten, what about the Brain Nugget? Surely it has to be stuck in a brain to work. Guess I'd just be shut off from seeing the Trail Planet.'

She stopped swimming and tread water. She spoke, "Don't worry about sharks. They do grow very large here. There are huge barracuda and squid too, but they have their natural and very most favored food species available in massive quantities, so humans are only extremely rarely attacked by predators in the ocean.

If I were to die, the Brain Nugget Program Control would know it and you would be connected to another Trail Planeton and continue learning."

'Okay,' I thought.

As we swam back to shore, gorgeous, light brown dolphins swam with us. Some are right along side and others whiz past us at about 30 mph. Some shot up into the air. Their skin glistened in the sunlight. Exciting.

On the beach Wanda lay drying.

'Is this heaven?' I thought.

She said, "No. We don't have much detailed info on heaven. Most believe it's real, but, like you, we don't know much about it. This may seem like heaven to you. There are problems here, but nothing like the problems of Earth. People get sick. There's lots of lightning. We have floods and storms. There's a lot of good here though. You'll see."

Being her is calm, not conflicted. She's right here, right now. I don't feel any physical tension. Sort of wish I could hear her thoughts, but maybe it's better that I only hear what she shares in speaking.

Wanda said, "Yeah, it's better. So I can just be your friend. I hope we'll be friends. It would be awful to be in this connection with some jerk you can't stand. I can tell when you're just thinking and not trying to talk to me. I've been host before for another Earth human."

'So you Trailors do this a lot? Has it been done a lot with Earthers?'

"No, you're the second one. I was host for the first one. She was very poor and lived in a place with a lot of conflict. Ethnic and racial hatred and fear and hatred based on some so-called religions were overwhelming in her culture. Often she dreamed of more peaceful places. I was asleep and experiencing her perceptions when she was severely injured by a bomb. It was bizarre for me to feel her pain and her life energy draining away. As she died, her thoughts were full of brilliant light and color. The pain was so intense that it overloaded her nervous system into shock. She could still think though. She worried how her children would get on without her. A deep peace occurred, then she died. I guess I've experienced a bit of the dying process to a point. It was painful, frightening and then gloriously joyous and peaceful."

'Sounds kind of rough.' I thought. 'I can guess a few places she might have lived.'

"It was sad, but she loved the experience of the Trail Planet. The Trail is a beautiful place with little to fear. She loved it. She wanted to come over. I'm very blessed to live here. You are blessed to see it. I hope you'll feel blessed."

Wanda stood and stretched. Picked up the thin light blanket she'd been sitting on, folded it neatly and put it in her shoulder bag. Drank some grapey, lemony drink. We walk away from the sea.

"You ready to travel the trails of the Trail Planet With Hammocks?"

'Sure!' I thought.

Through some dunes we walked. Fragrances were dreamy, sagey. This woman is in great condition. We slog up and down sandy dunes like it's nothing. I see distant flashes of light.

Wanda said, "Those lights mark water stations. A mirrored spinning sphere is on a tower. Blue-colored ones mean water only. Green ones mean water and food. After dark or when it's cloudy a bright light comes on inside the sphere. Light can come out of the sphere but not in, like those one-way mirrors police use in interrogation rooms. Solar and a little windmill supply the power for the light and other things at the stations."

'Cool.' I thought.

"Yeah." Wanda said.

Walked about an hour before seeing other humans. On a trail now. Looks like it became a trail from use. Nothing really marks it.

On the same trail as we are a fellow walks from the direction we are going. Looks really fit and tanned. Wears a great looking round light tan hat with a wide brim and ventilation. All his clothing looked comfy, loose coral shorts, functional but stylish. Most excellent looking hiking sandals and a couple colorful necklaces.

As we passed him, Wanda said, "Hi."

He said, "Ello."

I thought, 'Wanda, how is it you Trailors speak English?'

She said, "Two hundred years ago, Gus the Walker put forth the theory that English is the universal language. It could not be properly disputed, so it's all we use now. We use the metric system too.

Sparky please close the thought channel. I need to meditate a little while."

'Okay, bye,' I thought. 'Harpo.'

Satchmo opens it. Harpo closes it.

She walked to the water station. Took a long, lusty drink of water from a fountainhead that looked like a fish. The water is cool and pleasant tasting. On her strong legs we move to the doorway of a ten foot square hut. Over the door is a placard with one word on it, *Relax*. Once in, she slid a latch like those on port-a-potties at the beach. There's a single bed, a lamp table with lamp and a book. Gus, is imprinted on the cover. She adjusted the climate control. The little room quickly cooled. She adjusted the opacity of the windows to a romantic dim. Opened the book to a page that contained one small poem titled, 'Being Small Protects You From Dark Spirits'. Here it is.

'BEING SMALL PROTECTS You From Dark Spirits'

GOD IS LOVE, SO YOU can be small
    Make yourself small
    Make yourself tiny
    Make yourself itsy bitsy
    Make yourself weensie
    Tilst you can't be seen
    Nor heard
    Nor heard of

FLAT ON HER BACK, HER hands folded like a presented corpse, she closed her eyes and thought smaller, smaller, smaller until we were not there. Floating in total darkness, flashes of light shot through laser-like.

    'Pretty rotten cool,' I'm thinking.

Chapter 4

I Wake Up

I woke up and I'm peed oh 'cause I wanted to stay there. I liked it there. But I'm not sleepy now.

'Satchmo; Sparky, do you want to hear my thoughts while you're awake?'

"Yeah." I said.

Wanda had fallen asleep in the Relax Hut.

Seems only when we're both awake is there no communication link between us.

I heard her thinking a song,

'The blue sky is blue

The green sky is green

And I am somewhere in between'

She sang this over and over for about two minutes.

I said, "Wanda, please stop thinking that song. I like it but. . ."

She thought, 'Sure. Sparky, are you free today? I want to tell you some stuff.'

I said, "I don't have to do anything for a few hours."

'Good', she said. 'I want to tell you about Gus and what he wrote and marketed.'

"Sounds good to me." I said.

'I'll read some Gus writings to you later when I'm awake and you're asleep. But now I'll just tell you about him.

Gus started writing when he was fifty-three. He retired that year. His kids were grown. He was single. Gus was a wonderful painter. The profession he retired from was marketing. He'd had a wankishly successful career as a Master Marketer with a ghoulishly successful advertising firm. He received a handsome pension pay-out, about ten million dollars. After taxes he had about eight million. Trail Planet taxes aren't as insane as the United States of Earth taxes. So he was set for his basic needs. He retired about two hundred fifty three years ago. He wrote, painted and marketed his views and artwork until he died, about fifty three years after he retired. That was about two hundred years ago. In the last ten years of his life he saw his ideas coming to life in the human world on a grand scale. So, for about two hundred years Gus-View has held majority sway. The last one hundred years it has been practiced by the vast majority, maybe ninety eight percent. So the evil is a mere two percent and it readily squashed when it is identified.

Gus was a master marketer. Everything he promoted was for no financial gain, but it made money anyway.

He was fanatical in his belief that humans were capable of existing in a state far from evil. He was not so much anti-government, but he believed if people distanced themselves from evil, government would matter less and less. This was a strong selling point for convincing people to flee evil. He promoted the paradigm that the enemy of all is not other people, but the enemy is evil itself.

Gus put forth how to identify evil and what to do about it. Nearly all violence, domination and treachery is evil. To initiate violence is evil. Rapists, murderers and child molesters are killed immediately on verification. Most guilty of assault the same.

Gweebon scientists had solved the energy production problem before Gus's time. Our planet had many conveniences and exciting, fun developments were popping up all over. Great cars, games, boats and planes and boggling entertainment choices.

Gus said, "All this science and happy techno goodies, abundance and leisure don't mean squiddle if our spirits are only drawn to rank death."

He believed if he sought wisdom from God on recognizing and squashing evil, God would reveal to him recognition and squashing technique and how to share it. Gus dedicated the last fifty three years of his life to learning and teaching how to recognize and squash evil.

Gus said, "The more evil is squashed, the more freedom is revealed. As evil is removed, the Spirit of God transforms the human spirit."

Basically, Gus the Walker firmly believed that humans, with a little guidance and a few miracles from God, could be much nicer than they were. God did teach him evil-recognition and evil-squashing techniques and threw in a few miracles to help things along.'

" Marketing eh?" I said.

'Yeah, it's crazy that it worked. Before Gus 99.97% of marketing had been for promoting products, services and political campaigns. Gus worked to tip the scale and promote the good as he saw it. The more people practiced his suggestions, the more freedom and beauty emerged. I've read about the time before Gus and compared to the state of Trail Planet people now, well, I'm just happy to be living 200 years after the life of Gus.

He started his marketing with a koozie, a t-shirt and a bumper sticker. He designed a logo that went on everything he produced for the plan. His website name, gusdrops.com, was included on all his promotional products. On his first three products he placed the phrases;

Skip to Faith

And

Fight evil Make peace

He never stopped producing his first love, koozies, but he also produced TV and radio spots and billboards.'

I said, "So, Gus transformed the state of Gweebon with phrases?"

'Yes,' she said, 'Not just phrases, but phrases that worked. They worked, almost by trickery, in transforming human spirits from dark pride, fear, depression, violence and treachery, to faith, love, peace and humility, all the good stuff.'

"Now that's doin' somethin'!" I said.

'Sparky, I need to break our link. I need some rest. I get kind of excited teaching about Gus. It's what I do for polkas. The polka is like your dollar but they're much easier to get. I'm paid to talk about Gus and do dramatic readings of his poetry and writings. I am very much a Gus lover, some say fanatic. It's because some take the Trail Planet freedom for granted. Usually they mature to understand and appreciate Gus, but I've seen some those who called me a fool, fanatic or unbalanced zealot lured into evil and squashed.

I'll talk to you soon. Harpo.'

A few minutes later, 'Satchmo, hey Sparky, before I rest may I tell you about squashing?'

"Sure," I said.

'Okay, squashing is the ultimate punishment on the Trail Planet. It is the punishment for humans guilty of absolute evil which has been indubitably verified. Without getting to technical; three meter in diameter, ten ton disk of polished, oiled steel is lowered onto the the guilty human which is lying on a grate of super-strong steel. The body is pushed through the steel grate much like pasta from a pasta maker. The resulting pile of human body ground meat falls through the grate and into a three meter in diameter tub which has a plastic sheet liner, much like the liner for a cat litter box or like an enormous garbage bag.

The bag is placed into a 3000 degree celsius oven and vaporized. The squashing offenses are, rape, murder, child molestation, serious assault and robbery. So, in a nutshell, that's squashing.

"You've known someone who was squashed?" I asked.

'Yeah, crazy I know. There are only about a hundred squashings a year on Trail Planet and I knew one of the squashed. There were many more when squashing was first started. I knew him because they caught him for the rape and murder of another Gus presenter the same day he was trying to pretend to befriend me. We had walked a few kilometers together when the Trail Police apprehended him. I went to the squashing. It was amazing.

It was Gus who put forth the squashing offenses. Gus, in his wisdom from God also has much to say about how to resist the evil and keep yourself very, very far from deserving squashing. The technique for the individual to resist evil impulses is calledsquogging. Squogging is self administered. It is accomplished with faith, phrases, prayer, activity and learning.

I just thought you needed to know there is squogging. Those who learn and apply Gus's Evil Recognition and Self Squogging technique are rarely squashed.

I promise there is so much more to the Trail Planet than squashing and squogging.

Talk soon. Ciaoa, Harpo.'

My own thoughts came back to the fore. I was thinking how Wanda's thought voice is the same as her speaking voice. So sure, calming, confident but not arrogant. Surely light years from meriting squashing and on very light maintenance squogging.

'Hmmm,' I think. 'This squashing and squogging must resonate with me. I'm already thinking using these words.'

I'm a dry sponge ready to soak up more Trail Planet experience.

I cherish this moment, because within this moment, which I am holding as long as I can, I decide to retire from Stupentious Financial. Age and time served requirements were met my last birthday a few months ago in February, but I've been a little scared to retire, but now I'm not scared because now I have a hobby and a new friend and teacher from another planet somewhere. Likely I couldn't work anyway. I'd be sitting in my cubicle always wanting Wanda to Satchmo me. Whence I return to work, after my week at Grayton Beach Recreation Area in Florida, I will retire.

Time to pack for camping.

Chapter 5

A t My Campsite

GORGEOUS WEATHER. I love this place. Scrubby coastal trees and shrubs make every campsite fairly private. Blue and orange my tent is beautiful, big enough for six people. My hammock hung between two trees. It took a couple hours to set up my tent, the screen house over the picnic table, unload my kayak and set up my clothes line. With the greatest of ease my air mattress inflated using a wondrous pump that plugs into my van. Coffee pot is set up next to my impressive, brushed stainless steel two burner propane-bottle stove. Also in the screen house is my big plastic box with kitchen stuff in it, my empty cooler for fish filets if I get lucky and my other cooler for beer, wine and various beverages. Each site has a fire pit. Firewood I brought from home is concealed behind my tent, excellent seasoned Red Oak. Bright lime-green my beach cruiser bike sits by one of the hammock trees.

Wanda must be awake. I haven't heard from her in a few hours.

The scent of Beach Rosemary wafts through my camp home often. This scent must trigger endorphins or something. I always feel better when I smell it. It's early May, the weather is glorious this time of year in Northwest Florida; mid eighties by day, mid sixties by night.

It's Sunday. My drive here started about 2:00 am, so I arrived here about 9:00 am. It took a few hours to set up camp solo. Time for a nap. It's a little warm in the tent but I have a fan that makes it just right.

Examining the first lemon cream cookie of the five I'm about to eat, I appreciate the design on the cookie wafers of this sandwich style cookie. Something like a round flower or sun or energy field is in the center. Three smaller daisy-like flowers touch the central energy field at points that would prescribe an equilateral triangle if lines were drawn between them. Emenating from the central design are curly, swervy lines which are orderly and fill the remaining space on the wafer. Around the outermost edge are equally spaced dots. It was the Trinity and the universe.

I REMEMBERED A WRITING of Gus I'd learned from Wanda.
"If you reach a peaceful state you may lose friends."
First out loud, then in thought only I sing,

NOBODY KNOWS THE TROUBLE I've seen
Nobody knows my sorrow
Nobody knows the trouble I've seen
Nobody knows my sorrow

NOBODY KNOWS THE TROUBLE I've seen'

I'M ASLEEP NOW.

Chapter 6

R iding With Wanda

WANDA'S IN SOME SORT of vehicle now. A motorcycle but it's enclosed in a clear shell. Very sleek we cut through the air. There was no engine noise, just a slight hum from a power plant about the size of an average grapefruit. There's room for a passenger, but she rides alone save for my thoughts in her head. She rides through arid sage-brush country.

It smells great. We're on a very smooth, glareless highway. Only a little hilly rolly and there are snow-capped mountains maybe fifty kilometers away to whichwards we travel.

It looks kind of hot out there but we are in climate-controlled comfort. Off the main road we go on a trail.

I think, 'Satchmo, Hey Wanda. Where are we going?'

"Hey," she says, "to a glorious rock-mountainy, geo-thermal area. It's okay to ride on these trails as long as you don't go faster than a slow jogging speed. I like riding slow. Pretty soon we'll leave the bike and walk a trail I read about. I've never been there so it will be new for me and you."

'Kay,' I thought.

"You hear how quiet this motorcycle is. Trail Planet scientist determined a method to safely release nuclear energy from any dense matter. We can even compress sand, dirt or wood to a point that it can be used. This 'Energy Pellet Technology', is used in nearly everything that needs an energy source. This motorcycle will run twenty years on one pellet.'

'Cool,' I thought.

We made our way up the trail. Wanda stopped the bike and got off and pushed it off of the trail and leaned it against a rock. The trail was icy and rocky. I saw ice and snow on the rocks and plants but we were very comfortable.

I thought, 'Wanda, why are we so comfortable?'

She said, "I'm wearing a 'Comfortmax'. It covers my whole body and I can cover my face if needed. You can barely see it, it's so thin. It insulates perfectly and protects from rain, insects and minor scrapes. In most cases just wearing the cover without it turned on is adequate for comfort, but heat, cool and ventilation can be adjusted if needed. Turned on or not, it allows perspiration to wick off and evaporate, and the skin does breath and receive light properly. These are the greatest. You can go to places that are very cold and go to places that are very hot and thrive there comfortably."

'I want one of those,' I thought.

"Earth probably won't have this technology for three-hundred years and maybe never if they don't change the focus of their curiosity. Gus succeeded in encouraging the direction of Trail Planet curiosity and resources to produce ideas and products that are designed to enhance the human being. Earth has some of that but not near the amount and intensity needed to see the way.

I read about the near-miraculous things that happened when the minds of Trail Planetors began focusing on producing ideas and products that were to enhance the human being. It's in a book titled, 'Results of Gus Way', the author, a devoted lover of Gus.

Sparky, I need to be sure you understand that I don't worship Gus. I do love him, but I worship the Creator of the universe. I worship and depend on The Creator-Creator, The Creator-Jesus and The Creator-Love-Spirit. The Creator is source of all things groovy. Apart from The Creator one can only find gooberishness. Gus sought The Creator and The Creator used him."

'It's cold here,' I thought.

"Yes, it's twenty degrees farenheit."

'But we're perfectly comfortable. I love that Comfortmax suit.'

Wanda walked up the trail. She wears a small backpack. Her shoes are the lightest, comfiest shoes ever known. Walked at least an hour saying nothing. I just drank in everything she looked at; rocks, streams of water, icy on the edges. A large bird circled high in the sky. I thought of how renewing it is for me when I go to natural places on Earth and how I need to do it more.

"Sparky, you know how big the sky is? You know how the universe goes on and on? You know how subtle the processes of life are? You know how gargantuan the energies are in the universe?"

'Yeah,' I said.

"Well," Wanda said, "This is how big Gus dreamed and how big Gus wanted Trailors to dream and further.

Within the first ten years of serious concerted, dedicated squashing, dreams got bigger and bigger and better and better."

'You don't say,' I said.

"I do say, yes I do. You're only pretty as you feel you know? You're only stupid as you feel. You're only evil as you allow and if you're evil enough then you must be squashed. If you must be squashed you've got nothing to complain about. I'm telling you Sparky for life to be worth a crap, evil humans must be squashed.

Squashing is one of the major tenets of the book The Creator gave Gus The Walker to write. The title of Gus's book is, Gus Book. His book is considered by most to be not a new book of the Bible, but more like an additional gift, like receiving a free eight piece set of corn-on-the-cob handle with the food slicer you bought. The first sentences of the book are this: {The Creator told me to write. I was told to write anything, at least 25,000 words. The Creator said, "Write what you can write, because what you cannot write is forever unknown. Tell a story as bizarre as you can, because nothing you can imagine will be more preposterous than actual human history. Write about a world where high and noble squashing has been practiced worldwide for a hundred years.}

Within the first five thousand words of Gus Book, squashing offenses are described, as is squashing mechanisms and the squashing poem is presented. The squashing poem has been sung and accompanied with instruments in many different styles. This is the squashing poem.

THE TRAIL PLANET WITH HAMMOCKS

If you turn to evil
You know oh oh
You must be squashed
If you turn to evil
You deserve
To be squashed

NO SECOND CHANCE
You will surely be squashed

THE SQUASHING DISK is beautiful
A gleaming massive tool
Ten tons a droppin on you

THOSE WHO TURN TO EVIL
Become human pate
Squished through the sharp grid

HUMAN PATE VAPORIZED
In the glorious heat
Oh mingle pate vapor with fragrant sensual oils

YOUR BIO-MASS A FLOATING gas
Blowin' in the wind
How we love the scent

IF YOU TURN TO EVIL
You are squashed and vaporized

THE INCENSE OF SQUASHING
Blowin' in the wind
Let us all rejoice
How we love the scent

I SAID, 'YOU'VE TOLD me a lot about squashing. Do some Trailors think squashing is abused or over-uesed?'

She said, "Some think so or fear so, but I believe the authorities are very thorough and conscientous before giving the sentence of squashing. I am complete and vigorous supporter of squashing. An excellent film was produced that presents the dark evil pits the Trail Planet prisons were before the implementation of squashing according the Gus directives.

But enough about squashing. It's just a tool. Let's walk.

Isn't it funny that if we choose one way at a fork in this trail we may be eaten by a mountain lion, and had we chosen the other we may have met an angel or someone very funny or wise?"

'Yes,' I said, "that is funny. Are any of these possible?'

"Oh yes all of these are possible."

'Lots of mountain lions?' I asked.

"No, not so many. Anyway the Comfortmax has an option I switched on that sends out a sound that humans can't hear that is repellent to mammal predators. We should be fine unless we are unlucky enough to stumble onto a deaf adult mountain lion."

We both laughed.

We made our way on the mountain trail. Wanda smelled so good.

I said, 'What sort of essential oils are you wearing? It's dreamy, almost intoxicating mingled with this cool, clean air."

She said, "It's The Squashing Scent. I love it."

"Me too," I said.

Chapter 7

H igh on the Mountain

WANDA LOOKED AT A WATCH-like gadget. The screen read 2723 meters.

"This is a good place to camp," she said.

We had arrived at a flat area.

"The sunset should be great from here," she said.

She pulled something about the size of a bar of soap from her pack. Set it on the ground. Pushed down in the middle. It started to expand. When it stopped expanding it was a mat the size of a queen sized mattress but was only about two inches thick. She expanded a pillow and then a blanket in a similar way.

She said annoyed, "Fishwhack, I always forget to erect the tent first."

She pulls out a golf ball sized thing, presses on it and it expands into a ten by ten foot transparent tent. Complaining a little she pushes the mat, blanket, and pillow into the tent.

We lie on the mat and pillow and aaaahh, oooohh, wowzy, mowzy, flipzy doodle, it felt good.

The breezes pick up and clouds roll in. The sun, it seems, will set in two or three hours. Raindrops hit the tent. Wanda pointed out a mountain lion off to our left. A deep valley seperated us from the lion.

I thought, 'This is gorgeous living. This is thrilling and relaxing. Do you spend all your time in the wild?'

"No, not all. In a few days I have a Gus Conference where I'm scheduled to speak. One of my favorite coastal cities is where. A lot of trailors love the cities. There's wondrous art, music and other fun stuff in the cities. There's so much that's been done with the energy pellets. It's amazing. In the city Diter, where I'm going to speak, there is a massive, complex water fountain extraordinaire. You can be snugly secured in these transparent, cushioned balls and be thrown around on the water in crazy, random ways. It's big fun. The food is great too. Everywhere wonderful food and drink.

But here, isn't this great?"

Flocks of twenty and thirty birds flew across our view. They looked like flocks of Earth Cedar Waxwings. There is something extra powerful about waxwings. I don't know what. They turn some switch in my soul. These flocks did the same.

The mountains glistened in the light rain mixed with sleet. Sometimes bright sunlight broke through the clouds.

Wanda said, "Paradise or Gooberville; It's up to us."

I smiled at the thought and began to imagine the land of Gooberville. It was kind of easy.

She continued, "This is Gus's very second koozie phrase, no, no it's his very third

koozie phrase. The first was Skip to Faith, the second was God is Love, Paradise or Gooberville is the third.

Hey Sparky, give me a Harpo. I want to lie here and drift in my thoughts in this place for awhile."

'Yes, I will too. Harpo.' I thought.

So I'm seeing through her eyes and I feel her breathing. The rain makes a very light patter on the tent. Clouds sail by. Sometimes the wind goes gusty. Some evergreen trees grow from the rocky crags and some leafless shrubs and squatty hardwoods that look like bonsai trees, all are glistening with ice. I feel Wanda massauging her calves, then above her knees, then pounding her thighs with her hands karate blade hand style. Breathing deeply, but not strained, she oohs and aahs a little. The slight aches and pains she feels are like the ones I had when I was twenty. I'm fifty-five now and may be beginning some hereditary arthritis, but it ain't so bad. She did a posture arching her pelvis upward. Then she stepped out of the tent holding her pillow, looked at the same instrument that showed our altitude. She checked the temperature with it. Fifteen degrees farenheit. She read it in farenheit for my benefit. She set her Comfortmax suit to seventy-seven degrees farenheit and sat on her pillow. The trees hissed and lightly crackled in the gusty wind. Purple lichen glowed when the sunlight made it between the clouds. Clean air invigorated her body. A sense of the mass of all this rock struck me.

The wind blew hard, about sixty mph at times. Wanda closed her eyes and experienced the sound and feel. Somehow the tent held fast. Wanda swayed in the wind. She opened her eyes slightly and saw the light rain and sleet blow near sideways.

Wanda said, "The wind is on

There is nothing else to do

The wind is on

There is nothing left to do

The wind is on

And I love you

The wind is on and I love Gus

The wind is on I worship God

The wind is on and I love you ooh ooh too ooh ooh

I think she just kept thinking, 'The wind is on, the wind is on ...'

She sat and swayed, eyes looking straight ahead, lightly focused on a rock formation. The clean, cold air rhythmically entered her lungs. Her warm moist exhale formed a cloud.The peace I feel in her is so unfamiliar to me.

'Satchmo,' I thought.

"Yes Sparky," she said.

'What should I be learning from this?'

She said, "Nothing, I'm just passing time in peace. As for knowledge, wisdom, understanding; whatever God gives you is given you. Ask God for knowledge, wisdom and understanding.

Harpo please."

'Harpo.'

I did ask God.

God said, "Keep open all your eyes and ears. Shut all your mouths for awhile. Find the stream. Dive in."

Chapter 8

G rayton Beach Earth 1

THE TRAIL PLANET WITH HAMMOCKS

I woke at my Grayton Beach Earth camp a little sweaty. My stomach doesn't hurt but inside me there is a nagging, gnawing discomfort, a low intensity anguish. I think it's me trying to change. I see why old dogs don't learn new tricks, it hurts like hell.

I've mentioned I'm quitting tobacco again. I really enjoy smoking a lot. Each time I try to quit, my struggles for reasons humor me. It's a probabilities exercise. If I quit now my cardiovascular and pulmonary health may last X number of years more. If I quit now I may avoid hearing, "Sparky, we see spots on your lungs." Then again, it may not matter squat and I could just keep on enjoying smoking. A curious addiction it is.

Always feel a little bummerish when I first return from sensing the Trail Planet through Wanda. It's so peaceful and fun there and she feels so much better than I do.

I'll just have a wake-up beer, an Irish Harp Lager. My friends, Richard and Gail, produce these koozies, brand name 'Groovy Coolie Koozies'. I use one of my favorite of their koozies. Printed with white ink on Kelly Green is the phrase, "Life is artful, mirthful, but I'm not free". Don't bother asking them what it means.

The beer goes down tasty good. Of course I want a cigarette but I've been quit for almost three weeks now. So though I desire tobacco, I am not irresistably compelled to partake of the pleasant drug. So light alcohol on an empty stomach will just do. Besides resisting tobacco, I'm resisting food-for-fun, another of my favorite narcotics. Sometimes it seems my skin is turning inside out. So I sit, I drink, I stare.

My forhead resting on my left palm, I close my eyes. On inhale I think tick. On exhale I think tock. I feel the warmth of the sun through the dappled shade. I hear the sounds of birds and the buzz of the odd insect. Tick tock tick tock tick tock tick tock. Up goes the airplane down comes the clock. I've lost my feet but found my hands. Might I never be disturbed again.

I think, 'You see the issue don't you? You look and look and there's nothing to be found. So have a drink, sit, tick tock.'

I feel the heat of the sun. I see that sunlight is not yellow. It is more clear than the clearest mountain stream. For the first time truly I realize to get to Gus' View, to get to the Trail Planet you have to navigate through breakdowns. The soul of Gus, like the soul of Jesus was as tough as a new leather boot sole and as soft as fine cotton. Do you battle demons by force or faith? Do you know when they are vanquished? Can they always return? Is evil a condition of Earth like wind? Just as if there were no wind there would be no life on Earth, if there were no evil would it mean the same? I have another sip. Tick tock.

People glide by on bicycles.

The wind is on.

Chhapter 9
The Wind is on on The Trail Planet

I guess I fell asleep. I'm looking through the roof of the transparent tent on the mountain. The wind is howling.

'Satchmo.'

'Hey Wanda, everything okay?'

"Hey Sparky, yeah I think it's okay. Well it's okay if you don't mind dying in a mountain windstorm.

I don't think I'm going to die though. The wind is about seventy miles per hour. I put some extra stakes around the tent and lowered it. I think it will be okay. We'll see."

The tent is half covered in snow and ice but we're comfy cozy in the Comfortmax suit. So we just lay there and watched snow and debris fly over us. Most satisfying.

"Sparky have you understood there's nothing to fear? Have you placed the Milky Way's black hole next to a dragonfly in your mind and realized you have no idea how either came to be? Have you wondered which is a deeper mystery? Have you wondered how faith in Christ defeats evil?"

The wind slowed to a breeze. The snow and sleet stopped and the clouds were gone. She took her cushion out of the tent and sat on it on the ground. The light faded to pastels with sunset.

Wanda looked at the moon and said, "See the moon?"

'Yes, it's darker than Earth's.'

She said, "Yes, it's mostly dark lava and coal. We have another moon that is very bright but very far away. It will be visible soon. It's so bright and sparkly because it's almost all ocean and ice. It has an atmosphere similar to the Trail Planet. The biological life there is crazy rich. Trailors have explored it but not exploited it. It's so far away it looks like a giant star. There are a few incredible islands on it. You can vacation there but it takes many, many polkas to buy a trip. You can win a trip if you're lucky. I always enter my name in the drawings. You can go as a science helper or entertainer for the scientists also, if you're lucky. I've put my name in for that too, in case one of the lead scientists wants a Gus Presenter and guitarist and singer along. I keep hoping for the call."

The dark grey moon was low and loomed large on the horizon at about three quarter phase.

Full darkness is on and the stars are magnificent. It feels like we are in them not under them and could reach out and scoop them into her hand.

Wanda looked at the bright moon peaking over a ridge top and said, "Look, look it's the bright moon. We're so lucky. It's in full phase."

It's about a fourth the size of the Earth moon but bright and shimmery like a star. A well-defined circle of dark sky is around it because it's light overwhelms the stars.

She looked away from the bright moon and said, "Do you see those lights that move a little. Oh see, there's one streaking. And there, oh look a covey, a flock is streaking. Those are angels."

She looked here and there as different coveys and individuals flew leaving streaks of light, shades of greens and blues and reds and yellows. They sketched an abstract dove, an abstract cross and an abstract sun.

Wanda said, "See, see it's the face of the older Gus. Now they're changing it to look like the face of no one in particular. Maybe it's the face of God or Jesus. No one knows for sure. Oooh, I love to watch the angels fly. I love this so much.

Trailors have been able to see the angels fly for about a hundred fifty years. It started when most of the evil on the Trail Planet had been squashed and it's grown more and more common as more evil is squashed. It really is a glorious, beautiful, magical thing. Angels are all through the universe and always have been, but evil blocks our perception of them. Sometimes they'll talk to you. If you eminate little evil and God knows your faith is faith not dependent on miracles you can see them and hear them."

'Do humans become angels?' I asked.

"We don't know. We don't know if they were created as angels or some were created as angels and some were humans first. We know they are spiritual beings, but we know humans are spiritual beings too. We think angels have free will and can be banished to dreadful places or be consumed once God determines they have become irretrievably evil.

Sparky, do you see the light over on that ledge?"

'Yes, I do. It's pale blue outlined with pink and lavender.'

"Yes, yes, it's an angel, an angel that has spoken to me before. She helped me about a year ago when I was worried about having almost no polkas. Her name is Patches.

Quickly Sparky, teach me a sweet, loving Earth song about Jesus."

I thought, 'Umm, umm, okay okay, I've got one.'

I sang to Wanda,

'As the deer pants for the water

So my soul reaches out to you

Jesus you are my heart's desire

And I long to worship you

Jesus you are my strength my shield

To you alone may my spirit yield

Jesus you are my heart's desire

And I long to worship you'

"Oh good, good I like that. Sing it to me again and I'll sing along. Patches may like it and come speak to us."

So I did and Wanda sang aloud. We sang it slowly. Her voice is beautiful and textured with emotion. Patches moved closer. We sang the song again. Patches appeared beside Wanda. The light from Patches illuminated Wanda and all around her. Wanda bowed her face to the ground.

Patches said, "Hold your head high, you are full of love and grace."

Wanda said, "Jesus is the light and love of all the universe and all the heavenly places."

Patches said, "He is worthy of all praise. Wanda, have you learned ways to carn polkas?"

Wanda said, "Yes, dear Patches and I thank our God for great mercy and abundant guidance."

Patches said, "Hello Sparky. Your heart is very pure for a human of Earth. You are blessed of God to know Wanda and learn Gus Way from her and to see the blessings of the squashing of evil.

Hold out your hands Wanda, palms up and cupped like a bowl."

Wanda did.

Patches continued, "Wanda and Sparky receive fresh and stronger faith in The Creator, receive fresh and powerful wisdom from the Spirit of the Creator and life-affirming love from the Creator Jesus. Your hearts and bodies will sing like birds of the love from your creator. Your bodies will tingle with joy like otters, lilke dolphin as you swim, run, walk, dance, stand, ride and rest in the mighty creations of your loving creator. Accept this courage, love, peace and wisdom from the glorious, majestic, loving creator. Accept these gifts with deep, humble gratitude and from this moment forward remember to praise and pray at least once a day and when you do, pray in this way. 'Thank you loving creator for the gifts you have given me of your nature and please loving creator fill me more and more as much as I can handle with more of the faith I need to be equipped to be filled with more of your nature of love, of wisdom, of peace, of creativity and of more of the mysteries of You that I do not now know. More of you within me loving Creator. Please more of you, on Jesus' merit, through the love of your Spirit. Thank You Loving Creator.'"

Wanda said, "Sparky and I thank You Loving Creator for these gifts and for the gift of this prayer you have shared with us through Patches. Thank You Loving Creator."

Wanda's hands were full of liquid, colored pale green like sea water.

Patches said, "Drink most of the liquid from God, but save enough to drip in your eyes, sniff up your nose and drip in your ears."

As Wanda drank none spilled, the flavor stimulated all her senses; taste, touch, smell, sexual zones, from tips of toes to tips of fingers, to scalp, ears, nose and lips. It tasted like a finer wine than I'd ever known.

She snuffed some into her nose. She dripped some in her eyes. She dripped some in her ears.

Patches said, "Now drink the rest and lick it off your hands."

Wanda did. Her eyes stopped blurring. Her nose and ears dried. She looked and saw the nest of an eagle that she had not noticed in the light of day. She could hear small animals moving on a ledge far below us. She could smell the musk of an animal she had not smelled before.

Patches said, "You two are blessed more than many humans.

There are human worlds more free from evil than the Trail Planet and there are human worlds more evil than Earth. Those more evil than Earth are hideous places."

I said to Wanda, 'Wow.'

She said, "Wow indeed."

Patches flew away leaving trails of pinkish lavender graceful arcs toward the bright moon.

Chapter 10

The Wind is on on Grayton Beach

WANDA SAID, "SPARKY, that was beautiful. I am atingle with energy."

I said, 'Me too.'

She said, "There's a word to cut off our connection completely for a bit. If you don't much mind, I'm going to use it now. I need some time to savor what we just experienced."

I said, 'Sure, but how do we reconnect?'

She said, "There's another word. I'll use it in a few days."

I said, 'I'll talk to you then.'

She said, "Plundrum."

I slept like a baby cat for many hours.

My drip coffee maker is a wondrous luxury here at my campsite in the Grayton Beach area of Northwest Florida. I brought my electric coffee bean grinder too.

Fresh coffee brewed from freshly ground fresh, quality Columbian bean. Very good.

I couldn't get the song from the nineteen sixties, Patches, out of my head.

"PATCHES I'M DEPENDING on you son
    To pull the family through

41

My son it's all left up to you"

THIS IS FINE COFFEE.

Patches the angel was so much fun. I'm still atingle from the experience. More, I want more. I've never had an Earth angel encounter. I believe it happens on Earth, but it's rare, there's something retarding that experience. The Trail Planet has developed cleaner spiritual air.

Trying to remember the Prayer of Patches. Hmmm, Loving Creator, give me more faith, give me more of your love and wisdom and peace. I remember pray on Jesus' merit.

Three cups of coffee and a few lovely cheap cigarettes and it's time for a shower. Maybe I shouldn't have brought cigarettes.

On the way to the showers I see other campers at their picnic tables enjoying coffee. The smell of bacon drifts from some of the Camper Trailers and RV's. Some kids whiz by me on bicycles. The scents are wild and full of love here; the salty ocean air, the coffee and bacon, the pine and beach rosemary.

On the throne, as it's sometimes called, I was expressing my bowel when words and phrases came into my mind like boring beetles and laid eggs. I wanted to speak aloud and I wasn't sure if anyone else was in the bath house, so I opened my cell phone and pretended to dial. No one could see me in the throne stall so I tried to make a little noise when I flipped open my phone.

"Hello, oh hey Patches. What's going on?"

With enthusiasm I continued, "Oh I see, yes, oh yes, surely, no doubt, umm humm."

I pretended to listen for a minute or so, tossing in the occasional yeah and that's true.

"Yeah I'd like that very much. Sounds great. Excellent. Why didn't I think of that?"

I laughed and continued, "I'll talk to you later. Love you, bye."

I wanted to verbalize sounds because I was excited about the phrases in my head as if squirming larva by boring beetles laid.

Horrid wiping was fast, thorough and efficient. Which is not always the case.

The showers have room for you to remove your clothes and place them on the hooks and bench provided within the privacy of your curtained stall. Another curtain seperates the wetting area from the towel and clothing area. In this amazing zone I disrobed and turned the shower on low. I sat on the bench and wrote in the pocket-sized spiral notebook I always carry. I wrote:

CHEESE NITS FOR WANDA
No connections were missed
From conception to death
There were times I did put graves on flowers
Ranting in Paradise
There are cheese in my grits
There are nits in my rice
It's a long day in a short year

THE WATER TEMPERATURE was perfect in the shower splashing off my chest in America. I used my favorite mantra.

I thought, 'Ocean, ocean, ocean, ocean ....'

My eyes closed. A beautiful woman comes near me, Her smell is delightful. We communicate but do not speak. I am a giant in the vast space of God's mind. I am not conflicted. I am that I am madam.

Eyes open now I perform my ablutions.

Experiencing the Trail Planet does not make me bored with Earth as I would guess it might queerly.

To pass the time until Wanda opens our channel again, I'm going to walk long on the beach.

Chapter 11

Walk Long on the Beach

I got rhythm
I got music
I got my girl
Who could ask for anything more
This song is in my head while I walk the beach.

Surf rolling enough for sounds of glory. Seas maybe two or three feet. Low tide starting to turn around to creep its way back to high. Determined to collect only the most prize shells I survey the clusters of shells casually. Not many people about this Monday morn. It's about ten o'clock. My hiking belt holds two one liter bottles of water and has storage areas. In one of these areas I have four mini-bottles of Pinot Grigio, two nutrition bars, one pack of peanut butter crackers, a PayDay candy bar and a double-bagged quart baggie of ice.. Elsewhere in my hiking belt I have a tube of sun screen, cigarettes and a lighter. A large towel rolled longwise with its ends tied together with rope is draped across my torso like a bandeleer of rifle cartridges. Wearing my groovy waterproof hiking sandals my full-round brimmed ventilated hat, loose swimmy trunks, and a light long-sleeved pale blue cotton shirt. I'm set.

A windswept glorious day. Sun clean air walking. Walked a mile along the surfline. I found the perfect spot near a gnarled driftwood log. Illegally I walked in the dunes. Absorbing sun light near naked. Drank water and wine, snacked, prayed, meditated, napped, swam. I fantasized about a truly free world of humans and I thanked God that I get to see one. I speculated on what I will see hear feel and learn on the Trail Planet.

I'm blessed and lucky as a puppy born into a dog lover's home. I've got the lub down in my soul. Learning the Trail Planet is showing me the freedom I have on Earth.

I'VE BEEN UNAWARE OF my bindings

Now I see them and tear at them resolute and fierce
I am spirit in flesh
Squalls far out to sea
Sometimes a fish feeding frenzy near shore
Pipers, plovers walk the surfline
Gulls,terns search and dive
Pelicans dive and rest
The wind is on
The sea is brilliant

WHEN I EAT TOO MUCH it's like a self-inflicted depression, a self-inflicted illness or wound. I'm thinking about this because yesterday and today I have eaten just enough and I feel fine. Two bottles of wine down and I feel fine.

Dolphin are feeding and playing nearer the beach than they should with no helmets. I love that they are so close. So fit, so gorgeous, so sleek, so glistening tan. They burst up through a massive school of Spanish Mackeral, several with flapping blue, green, purple irridescent mackeral in their smiling, spikey teeth. They fall back to the water with a smacky splash. Their thrilled energy is contagious. Energy from them courses through me. I am in love with them.

Then with a splap and a thud one of them plops three feet onto the beach. She flops wildly, with mackeral still firmly in her jaws.

She was squeaking and cackling as if to say, "Oh shite, this ain't good."

I walked to the dolphin and said, "Oh shite, this ain't good."

Tense seconds passed. She calmed herself. Prostrate, she appeared to be searching her mind for a solution. She flipped her mackeral in the air a few inches, caught it and gulped it down. Her head nodded up and down.

She opened her mouth and said, "Eee, eee, eee, eee, eee."

I scavanged a plastic beer cup from The Sultry Parrot, a local bar. Pictured on the cup is a great image of a parrot with sultry eyes and a you're in my power smile. With this cup I poured water onto the planted dolphin while I considered my save-the-dolphin strategy.

The group she was with stayed near. Dolphin heads popped up just past the breakers and they laughed.

"Hang on BB," I said.

I named her BB because she was as lovely as Bridget Bardot in her twenties. She may have been male for all I know but she seemed female with her fetching eyes, smooth tan skin and that flipper, oh my.

Her breathing was calm as though she had confidence that I could help her back into the Gulf.

I tugged on her tail. She did not budge. My knees bent, I tried for maximum pull. Her tissue seemed to stretch. I felt or heard a slight crackling. I prayed it was not coming from my back. As I pulled she jerked in a swimming motion. Her tail came free of my hands and I fell backward into the surf. The dolphin heads laughed louder. Together, BB and I had moved her six or so inches closer to the sea. The tide was coming back in and the squall was nearer us. The waves were getting larger and the water poured around her with each wave that reached the beach. I gripped her tail again and waited, watching the incoming waves like a surfer. This one, this one, no. This one, this one, yes. A wave a third bigger than the others rolled in. I held tight. It lifted BB about an inch and it tried to push her further up on the beach. I held fast and pulled her seaward, maybe ten inches. Water moved around her about two inches deep now. She wiggled and flopped. Her flopping moved her in the wrong direction.

I jumped in front of her, my hands in the universal stop position, I said, "No BB no! We are nearly there. Cease, cease your struggling. This is not your hour. Please be calm."

Held my hand just over her blow hole. Her exhale was warm. I leaned over to smell her breath, the scent of sea air with a subtle fresh fish bouquet.

Waves are building as the squall approaches. Light rain arrives with lightning and thunder.

I take my position aft and secure her powerful dolphin tail in both hands. Pull and rest, pull and rest. We gain about a half inch, then an inch, then two, four, six, eight. The dolphins are laughing and cheering. She's in a foot of water now, moving back and forth like an alligator. Out, out, out into the sea we go. I step into a washed out spot of the sea floor. Falling backwards, I still grip her fluke. Under the water I go pulling her over me. Fully in the water now she fires up her mermaid undulations and whack my feet that have popped up out of the water. She swims out to join her group. The squawk and cackle their gratefulness to me. About thirty yards offshore they give me a grand jumping exhibition.

Dancing, jumping and hollering I celebrated on the beach, sharing the moment with the dolphins.

"Thank You God," I yelled to the sky over the sea with my arms raised high in the air.

"Thank You God."

"BB lives."

I continued my celebration with peanut butter crackers and wine after I'd floated and paddled around awhile to cool down.

Several hours on the sand, I'm beginning to roast a little, so I put on my long, loose, light clothes once I'd air dried.

Chapter 12

Walk Long on the Beach Back to Camp

The walk to my spot on the beach, the sight of BB's rescue, was further than I thought. I thought it was one mile, it was more like four.

Mostly I looked just in front of me as I trudged my way back to camp. Looking up once at a Great Blue Heron near the surf line just ahead of me I saw in my peripheral vision a figure walking out of the dunes. This figure in orange and white appeared to be setting a course to intercept my path. I'm not overly paranoid but my caution juices stirred a little. Further along I could tell the figure was a female. I trudged ahead more relaxed since psychotic thieves, rapists and killers are, by a large margin, predominately male. The nearer we approached intersection I could see she was a quite attractive female and I saw no male, female or child potential companions in the area. She was right away interesting to me.

"Hello," she said. "I was sitting in the dunes looking around with my binoculars and I saw you saving that dolphin. I wanted to come and help but I was too far away. Good job."

I said, "Yes, it was fun. I'm sure she would have done the same for me. My name is Sparky."

I offered to shake her hand. She seemed a little reluctant but did shake my hand.

"I'm Fran."

I checked for wedding ring. She wore none.

"Do you live nearby?" I asked.

"No, I love it here though. I come here when I can. I'm staying in a cabin in the park."

"Ooh, I like those," I said. "I stayed in one for most of a week once. Had to leave a few days early because of Hurricane Ignatious. I love the screened porches they have in back.

I have a tent set up in the campground, so I guess we are neighbors. It's just me, my coffee pot, my stove, my screen house, my coolers, my bike and my kayak.

Are you here with family?"

"No, just me," she said.

I said, "I was on my way back to camp. Would you like to come with me and have a wine or beer?"

"Sure," she said.

So we made our way.

Fran is a strong walker. I love that in a woman or any human for that matter. I'm a strong walker but I quickly tire because I take with me everywhere a thirty pound male fat belly pack.

"What do you do for work?" I asked.

She said, " I don't work anymore. I used to be a court reporter. I was very good on the funky little typewriter.

I've no children. I am a widow. I like saying I am a widow, not that I didn't love my husband. I did love him. It's just that the word widow is so pleasant to say and so loaded with poetic incense."

"Poetic insence, I like that. I am a widower, Which is a strange word also. I love my wife very much. I say love because I believe she still is. I have secret conversations with her. She may actually still be alive biologically. She disappeared during a botanical research trip to the Amazon. Since there is no evidence of how and where she disappeared, I have two preferred beliefs. One, and I give this one the most credence, is that she ascended into heaven like Enoch. The other is that she drank a tea made from hallucinogenic plants with the Shaman of a beautiful tribe of native Amazonians and during the experience she and the Shaman believed they had a visitation from The Great Creator and The Great Creator told them that she must stay with the tribe and be treated as a treasure from heaven and she must be hidden from all outside the tribe and The Great Creator told her that I would be all right.

I did actually receive a letter signed, Sincerely, The Great Creator, which stated, and I paraphrase; Your wife is hidden with a beautiful tribe and her life is mightily blessed and joyful. You will receive a manuscript from her in the future but you will not see her again in your

Earth body. Love, The Great Creator. There was a PS that said; Just kidding, your wife ascended into heaven like Enoch.

Of course I thought it was a cruel prank so I did some research and analysis of the letter and envelope. Turns out the font used is unknown, has never been seen, the chemicals in the ink could not be identified, the material of the envelope and letter could not be identified, burnt, dissolved, torn, cut, lasered or in any way altered. I believe it is a letter from The Great Creator. I have hidden the letter and envelope securely away."

"That is something," Fran said.

"Yes it is," I said.

Finally I arrived at my campsite. Sat at my picnic table under my screen house, opened a Liberty Ale, an excellent ale from San Fransisco and thought about my day on the beach. I remembered rescuing BB the dolphin as being a real experience. A beautiful, soaring marine mammal, love wonderment. Meeting Fran had been a hallucination. My mind is being a trickster in me. This ale is excellent and this cheap cigarette satisfying. The Brain Nugget maybe the cause or maybe it's my experience of being within Wanda as she meditates. Maybe I'm still grieving from losing my wife. Did I lose her or did she leave? Did she die or abandon me, moving to St. Lucie with a wealthy professor? I can't say.

AFTER THREE LIBERTY Ales I ride my lime-green beach cruiser bike to the shower house.

Refreshed from my shower I drink three more wines, write this poem and go to sleep.

I FELT I WAS FALLING but I was not

Did the Earth hesitate a second in it's spin

I think maybe
Or a star in our galaxy decided to stop orbiting the center for a
moment
Or God revised the plan for me
Or maybe all three

Chapter 13

Wanda and Grundle

I SLEEP VIGOROUSLY, needing it more than I needed anything.

Wanda is looking at a handsome young man who is speaking to her. His face is serious, nearly scowling.

Very quietly, hoping Wanda would not hear, I thought, 'Satchmo.'

"I've loved you for years now. When I see you you're sweet to me, like you care about me. I think you do care about me but not enough to want to be with me," he said.

Wanda said, "I do care, but you're right, I don't want to be with you like a couple or have children or any of that. I like you, I like to talk with you and sometimes hold you but I'm not in love with you Grundle. I've told you that over and over. Now go away. Don't contact me. If I want to speak with you I'll call you."

As he walked out the door he said, "Don't bother."

"Sparky," she said a little pissed sounding, "Did you enjoy that?"

'It wasn't fun but I think I'll be okay.'

She looked in a mirror so I could see her and said, "Funny, Earth boy."

I thought, 'Bite me, Trail Planet smarty pants know it all.'

She smiled then laughed and placed her hands together like praying hands then each middle finger protruding through and flapping out of rhythm like spastic bird's wings she said, "Double-bird humpster, earthworm."

I thought, 'You've got me there, monkey-feet.'

She was still smiling. She laughed a little.

I laughed a little and thought, 'and hands.'

She stared at the mirror feigning anger. Then we both laughed loud.

She said, "I love Grundle, in a way, but he's too serious. I don't want a special man friend. I had a perfect love for fourteen years. I'm not searching. I'm satisfied. Since I've been able to study and experience Earth, I think I have a deeper appreciation of the freedom on The Trail Planet and I love it. I need not a whiney man nor a near-perfect fellow. I revel in the animals and the humans here. I like talking to you too."

Wanda is a gorgeous woman, maybe forty years old. I mean she is Victoria's Secret exceptionally wondrous in form and face. I'd have to work hard not to look like a blathering idiot if I got this much attention from her on Earth in four deminsions.

Chapter 14

Wanda and Me in the City

'IS THIS YOUR APARTMENT?' I asked.

"No, it's just a nice hotel room that the company I'm speaking for tomorrow got for me."

She looked out the window. We were on maybe the fortieth floor. The sun just a few fingers above the horizon. Our view is of a bay. Water taxis move over the smooth water and birds fly.

Wanda sprayed a maddening sensual scent on her neck and hair, like sandalwood sweetened with a light strawberry and vanilla. She looked in the mirror and ran her fingers through her just-washed hair to help it air dry. Her hair light brown and naturally streaked by the sun. She rubbed a light moistening oil on her arms and face that made her tanned skin shimmer. She wears a sheer soft cotton sun dress that is pale blue with a coral tropical flower print on her right hip. Two inch ear rings of pink coral and small white feathers dangle by her cheeks. This woman is gorgeous to behold and her spirit is sweet as a cool summer rain. Am I in love with her? Oh yes, but that is futile as bitterness or dipping water with a net.

"Okay Sparky, let's go out on the town."

'You are a beautiful woman,' I thought.

"Yes I am, by American Earth standards and I'm pretty cute on the Trail Planet too.

Gus says, "Beauty or any other gift is like cat fur on a frog if the soul is in death rot."

'Hmmmm,' I thought.

The elevator is spacious and padded, dramatic ambient music plays.

Wanda said, "This is fun."

Each passenger got into individual stalls that were all around the circular elevator car. It would not move until each passenger strapped into a harness attached to the floor. Once all were secured the elevator car released and dropped in free fall and everyone was weightless until we hit a blast of air that gently slowed the fall. I felt Wanda's delight as she floated, her firm tanned legs exposed. There is a carnival ride thrill in her stomach. Wanda looked at the tanned strong legs of another female passenger who floated. She wore turquoise colored panties.

"I love that. Did you like it?" Wanda said.

'It was great.'

"Let's walk Sparky. We'll go to the Food Land Zone soon."

'Where are we?' I quizzed.

"We're in Angels. I know you have a Los Angeles on Earth. But this is just Angels or Angeles."

"It's groovy, doovy, keeno here. I do love the wilderness but I love the cities full of people too."

Wanda walks the street past club entrances where pretty people sensuously dressed invite her in promising that it is glorious paradise experience inside. Some of the hawkers are striking young women dressed tight and scanty. They don't seem cheap or flaunty. They seem more wondrous beauties in nature. I would've gone into the first one, but Wanda walked on by.

Some people on the street said, "Polkas please. Please some Polkas."

Wanda mostly ignored them.

I remembered that on Earth I'm the biggest sucker for panhandlers when I'm in a big city. I think they see a sign over my head that says – Goober will give dollars, stupid, approach with confidence. I can't go to big cities much. I did finally learn to carry no cash, so I could honestly say I've got no cash and at that time the panhandlers had no hand held debit card processors, which of course, they have now. I did finally learn to say, I have no cash and no debit or credit card, God bless you brother or sister. Wanda just walks past them all.

She says, "It's fairly easy to get Polkas here on The Trail Planet so I have little compassionate concern for the drug and alcohol addicts that are asking for Polkas."

I thought, 'Is addiction a major issue here on The Trail Planet?'

Wanda said, "Are we getting solicited more or less than on Earth?"

I thought, 'Less I'd say.'

She said, "Addiction and sluggardlyness is still a problem here but not too bad. I have a rule that I never give them anything. We have so many generous shelters for food, drink, even wine and the teachings of Jesus and Gus that I don't worry about them. I just say, God loves you or nothing or skip to faith and I just walk by. They won't get angry and assault me because they know, even though they're drug addled, that if they assault me physically or try to steal my money or even verbally assault me, they may be squashed.

I love squashing. Squashing has done more for this planet than I can tell you. Squashing is divine. It's always time for the good the right to stand and be loved and adored and for evil to be called evil and be without hesitation or consternation be squashed. Squash it. Squash evil every time. I don't give a shite or a drivvle, squash it, squash it. You know what I mean?

I thought, 'Damn straight I'm with you Wanda. Squash it. Evil is squashed every single blinkin' time it's exposed. Squash it squash it. I love you. I love Gus. I love Jesus. I love you.'

Yes I said it. I love Wanda. I want to give her pleasure on Earth or The Trail Planet or any where by God's will I can. I love this person with all my heart. I need her. I desire her. I am a foolish Earth man and I love this being. I will follow her to hell because I know she knows the way out.

Wanda ignored my proclamation. She walked into a dance club. Sort of Techno music was playing. These lyrics repeated over and over, (I couldn't worry if I tried).

WANDA SAID, "DO YOU know what faith is?'

It was still and quiet for a long time, like three or four minutes.

Then Wanda said, "Now you know. It's still and quiet. It's listening to the hum of the stars."

She walked in among the dancers. Of course, she danced naturally and lithely, her arms flowed up and down with grace. Some people danced as couples, but most just danced solo with the occasional glance at another dancer as if to dance with them. Many of the dancers were young, athletic and beautiful, but some were older and a little stiffer, but only a few were very fat. There were some people in wheelchairs dancing using their hands, heads and arms.

Wanda danced about twenty minutes then went to the bar and sat. She ordered a Tequila Happy Jack and crab dip with nachos. The Happy Jack tastes a lot like a margarita and the crab dip was limey, garlicy and peppery. The Happy Jack has something in it other than alcohol that induces euphoria. She ordered five cigarettes. They taste like tobacco but smell like marijuana. Wanda is having a good time, so, so am I.

I feel a touch on Wanda's shoulder.

"Hi Wanda," he said.

"Banyin, oh Banyin," she said. "I haven't seen you for so long. How are you?"

She got up from the bar and they hugged and hugged. He held her very tight and I felt a stirring in her stomach and a flushing of her neck and cheeks and a tingle in her loin. I think women have loins.

"I've missed walking with you," he said.

Banyin is very fit and his skin is olive-tan and his hair a light sun streaked brown like Wanda's.

"I've loved walking alone," she said. "But sometimes I miss talking and cuddling with you."

"Wow, you look great," he said.

"You too," she said. "Sit with me, or are you with others?"

"I'm here alone."

"Why are you in Angels?" Wanda asked.

"I saw on the GusTalk website that you are speaking here tomorrow. I got my ticket early so I got a great spot.

I wanted to hear what you've understood of Gus lately and I hoped to see you. I came to this club because I remembered you liked it here. God is so love. I'm happy to see you."

"Excuse me a second," Wanda said to Banyin and continued, "Sparky, can we Harpo for a little while. I'm getting a lot of garble with all your thoughts coming through."

I thought, 'Sure, Harpo.'

I had been thinking a lot about who is this Banyin? What's his significance to Wanda? That sort of thing.

Gently I thought, softly singing like a lullaby, 'Satchmo.' So's I could listen.

Wanda turned away from him as if to cough and she whispered to me, "I know you Satchmoed."

I listened.

He asked, "Are you married or have a special man or anything?"

"No," Wanda said. "I'm not looking really. Not much interested in such."

"There is no other Tree," he said.

"Yep," she said.

He said, "I'm forever grateful you tried with me for that year. It was great. I'll always be in love with you," Banyin said.

"I'm glad I tried too. You mean a lot to me. You helped me get to a livable grief after Tree's death.

I'm so absorbed in Gus now. It's my calling to communicate Gus to people and just be free."

"You're so good at Gus. I've listened to all your recorded presentations.

Where is your baby girl now? Do you see Treeny very much?"

"She's my twenty year old baby now. She lives mostly in different places on the Storied Coast. She paints and sings and plays guitar for Polkas. She is beautiful. I go see her about a week each year."

He said, "She is so sweet, an angel. She fits the Storied Coast. What a magnificent place."

She said, "Yes, the sand beaches and the pebble beaches are angel favorites. Different flowering plants on the rolling hills are wild with color most of the time.

What have you been doing.?"

"I'm still working in Brain Nugget Science. It's getting better and better. There are about a thousand hosts now.

We're hosting a lot more Earthers. I know you hosted that lady on Earth that was killed."

"I'm hosting an Earth man now. The part of Earth he lives in and how he thinks gives me more hope that hosting Earthers isn't a waste of time. He has faith and is fairly self-contained. His name is Sparky."

I didn't pay much attention to their conversation. I wondered about Tree. It reminded me when I was a Southeastern USA hippy boy. There was a hippy girl named Leaf that seemed to float about on my community college campus. She could speak but she seldom did. My good friend Torbin and I both wanted to befriend and romance her but in our own way each of us stimulated no interest from her. When we tried to greet her or engage her all we would receive in return was a smile of pity. She was so spirit-like that she wore a jingle bell anklet. I think the tinkling of the bells reminded her that she was indeed on a physical plane and reminded her not to float or fly and alarm us dirt people. She was a perfect hippy beauty; shiney straight brown hair, smooth olive tan skin, slender but feminine hips, wondrous young breasts that peaked from her colorful halter tops. She had the perfect body for the hippy hip hugger bell bottom low waist band jeans. A few inches of her flat tummy shone like a beacon. Her legs so sleek, her face and her seldom heard voice euphoria inducing like Wanda's. I wanted know what traits would I need to arouse the interest of a woman like this.

I wondered what made the deceased Tree the love of Wanda's life. The one she'd rather spend her life remembering instead of sharing her beautiful spirit with someone still alive. I wanted to learn more about Tree and from Tree. I wanted to know how he died. I wanted to know more about Treeny too. I marvel at these things like I marvel at the sun. Surely our spirits go on forever. Only that makes sense to me.

I wondered, I guess aloud in my thoughts, 'God do our spirits go on forever? Is the starting point human birth then we go on forever?'

Wanda said, "Yes Sparky that's true."

Then she told Banyin, "I think I love this Earth guy Sparky that I'm hosting. He's so close."

I nearly melted. She must have whispered a Satchmo.

Banyin said, "He must be a remarkable Earther. From what I've heard Earth is a hard place to see the real."

Wanda said, "I think, yes, he may be remarkable."

Wanda loves me.

"You want to dance?" Banyin asked.

"Sure," she said.

They put on music and danced and danced. The song had these lyrics.

I love you I love you I love you
I love being free with you
I love being free without you

These three verses over and over with frequent instrumental breaks.

Wanda moved so smooth and lithe, light sensuous and fluid with her strong thighs and healthy feet.

Something kicked in, some narcotic, maybe just alcohol, but, I think alcohol plus. Inhibitions were falling like feathers.

Euphoric feelings growing like a sweet fragrance. Banyin danced like a virile man that knows just how suggestive of sex to be with a woman he desires and who is showing signs of reaching that delicate equilibrium thoughtful women must reach before sliding into mutual abandon.

A stirring welled in Wanda's belly and below as she glanced at his rising desiring. He sensed her stirring, moved in closer and put his arms around her. He smelled good like rain in a fir tree forest with a little patchoule musk. Wanda stirred further and her legs went a little limp, her cheeks flushed. He's much more physically fit than I, younger, smarter, a brain-nugget scientist. His work brought me together with Wanda so I tried not to be too angry that he was likely about to oompa loompah my love.

Banyin said, "May I come to your room and share some wine?"

Wanda just squeezed him a little tighter, saying nothing, they walked out.

In the room there was wine in a small refrigerator. Banyin uncorked the wine with little effort with his strong hands. Wanda lit a jasmine candle she pulled from her bag and turned off the light. She turned on the sound system that sounds like the best I'd heard on Earth. It played some smooth instrumental jazz-like stuff. He poured the wine. They sat on a large couch. Not a word was spoken. They each drank some wine. Then he kissed her gently, their tongues lightly touching, saliva lubricating their lips. They kissed like this for many minutes. They touched only at their lips. They stood and removed their clothes. Wanda lie on the couch. He took a sip of wine and held it in his mouth. He positioned his mouth over her fragrant tropics and let the cool wine drizzle onto warm moist cache. I think a little steam rose. Her body moved spontaneously. Ecstacy flowed through her whole body. His mouth reached her tropics. I'm advanced in this skill so I appreciated his skill in this activity. Wanda was in the highest human body pleasure.

Then I woke up.

Chapter 15

F ran Stalks an Oaf

TURNS OUT FRAN WAS not a hallucination. The brain nugget had given me the impression that something real was not real. Living through Wanda, who loves me, on the Trail Planet and still living in my fifty-five year old male body on Earth kind of confuses my perception of real, dream and fantasy. I still have actual human sleep dreams. Wanda said I should not go too long with no dreaming or I would likely go insane.

Fran happened by on her turquoise beach cruiser after I'd snuck into the wild shrubbery to pee and I'd brushed my teeth at the campsite water faucet. I was nearly finished with my first cup of fresh ground Columbian coffee. It's the day after BB's rescue. I'd slept through thunderstorms and through the night.

"Good morning Sparky," she said in the tone a confident woman uses when she's interested in you.

"Hello," I said, "I like your bike. It's pretty."

She said, "Your coffee smells great."

"I'd love you to join me," I said.

She stepped into my screen house.

I said, "I had decided that meeting you yesterday was not a real event. Weren't we supposed to have a beer together?"

"Yes," she said, "But you scared me a little with your theories on what happened to your wife. So while you were looking at a bunch of dragonflies feeding on white aphids rising off a bush, I slipped away."

"That could be understandable," I said.

"I actually know how she died but I prefer my fantasies. I don't know why I told you my alternate realities. Kind of wierd, don't you think?"

"A little," she said, "But also fascinating." with that tone of voice again.

I said, "My wife died from an allergic reaction to a medication used to treat Nasty-Green-With-Orange-Specks-Fly Fever. This fever has symptoms as miserable as malaria and worse. She was only on a two week expedition. I stayed home and worked and kept up with the kids.

They told me she said, "Tell Sparky I love him and thank God for him and our beautiful children."

She had more blessings for the kids too.

If she couldn't recover I'm glad she didn't have to suffer too long. She is glorious and wondrous.

How did your husband die?"

"Car wreck," she said.

We shared a moment of silence for our much-loved deceased spouses.

I said, "The humidity is low for down here. It feels great this morning."

Bugs weren't too bad so we took our coffees outside the screenhouse and sat on comfy folding chairs, using my large cooler for a table between us. We faced away from the camp road looking over a brushy area. Red-winged blackbirds sat on prominent perches displaying, trying to attract mates. An osprey soared through on it's way to fish and assorted birds cheeped as the sun lit up this piece of the Earth one more time.

"Do you have plans for today?" Fran asked.

"No," I said. "I know I won't sleep for a long time. I slept about eighteen hours last night I think."

"Are you ill?" she asked.

"No, I don't think so. I was just unusually tired."

I tend to tell people I've just met everything about myself too quickly. But this time I resisted the urge. If my stories about my wife's death frightened her, I thought, telling her that when I sleep I experience life on another planet as if I'm in the body of a beautiful musician, speaker woman, might be too much too soon.

Fran took one of my Seneca light one hundred cigarettes and lit up without asking, which I thought was very cool, even sexy.

"This is a pretty good cigarette," she said.

I said, "And they're really cheap, which makes makes them considerably less unhealthy. They're all tobacco, no deadly additives."

"I've done what I thought was impossible," she said. "I've become an occasional smoker. I'm not completely deprived of rich tobacco satisfaction and I feel in control and have less side effects."

"Cool," I said. "I'm working toward that level, but currently I'm a full-blown addict. I'm more concerned right now with being so fat around the middle. Sometimes I feel like a fat lunking oaf."

"You are a little fluffy," she said. "but not too bad. You're attractive enough in the classic sense and in the oafish sense. That's good for you, because some women may be attracted to your classic magnetism and others to your oafish appeal."

I laughed.

We spent the whole day together. We rode bikes until it got too hot. Then Fran went to her cabin to shower. I went to one of the campground bath houses and showered. I cleaned every nook and cranny of my glorious, sexy, oafish incarnation. Once dried I applied the perfect amount of my patchouli, sandalwood, musk, with a hint of honeysuckle concoction of essential oils. Only my favorite hibiscus print shirt would do for my evening with Fran. On a background of light tan it has light orange and burgandy shaded hibiscus. I wore my comfiest soft cotton light khaki shorts and my Sperry thongs my kids gave me on a Father's Day. You could grill a thick Red Snapper filet on me, if you know what I mean.

Fran picked me up in her pale-green convertible turbo-charged Saab, one of the older, cooler ones, in immaculate, like-new condition.

"Love your car," I said.

"It's a lot of fun," she said. "Do you want to drive?"

She opened her door and I was staring at her sleek tanned legs as they parted as she turned to get out of her seat.

I said, "No thanks, you drive for now if that's okay. I'll just enjoy the ride for now."

She said, "Let's go to Happy Snappy's Dock Café for lunch. We can sit on the deck and watch the boats come and go."

"Great," I said. "Let's go."

We ate salads and boiled shrimp and drank Margharitas.

Back at her cabin we made love, oily love. She had some edible, extra virgin coconut oil. We made love to the rhythmic sound of the surf. Moonlight and one lightly scented jasmine candle lit the bedroom. Covered in light sweat and sticky with fluids we lay there about ten minutes after we had spent ourselves in a forty-five minute intense charged excited state.

I said, "Wow."

She said, "That was lovely."

I said, "Yeah, it really was."

Fran said, "Would you please walk back to your campsite now?"

I put on my clothes and walked to my campsite. The stars twinkled nicely and small puffy clouds glided across the near-full moon.

I thought, 'I like this woman.'

Chapter 16

M agic Wanda Speaks to 80,000

I FELL ASLEEP JUST in time. Wanda was backstage looking over notes for her speech.

I thought, 'Satchmo.'

"Hi Sparky," she said. "What have you been doing? You've been away for awhile."

"Yes," I said. "I met a fascinating woman named Fran. We spent most of the night together."

"Yes," Wanda said. "I was asleep during part of your time together so I experienced what you experienced. I like her. She's very beautiful and a little mysterious. The oil and candle light were ooh la la."

I thought, 'Yes they were.'

Wanda said, "Did you like Banyin?"

I thought, 'He seems to appreciate you and appears a wonderful fellow.'

Wanda said, "Yes," and continued. "I'm about to speak to eighty something thousand

people who are here mainly to hear me speak."

I thought, 'I'm glad I'm with you to experience this. You must be a super speaker.'

"I'm not so great at speaking," she said, "but it seems I understand Gus as good or better than anyone and Gus understood, in the short time he was in a body that could write and speak that he should write

71

and speak so I write and speak. He understood the essential thing. He opened his heart wide to God's instruction and devoured it and obsessed on it like a dog eating warm, juicy beef roast. I have the excessive privilege of talking about Gus. An angel told me when I was a young girl that if you love Gus and study his writings, then you love Jesus and you love The Creator, or any combination of loving these three equals the same. So speak up little girl Wanda."

I thought, 'That's beautiful and I understand.'

"I know you do Sparky," she said. "You are an odd Earth person. You know I love you don't you?"

I thought, 'Yes, Wanda, I do and I love you.'

She said, "I know you do, which means you love Gus, which means the rest."

'Yes.' I thought 'Yes, Wanda'

"Read this Sparky. This is what, for the most part, I'm speaking about tonight."

She opened a large print Bible to Ecclesiastes and she focused her eyes on chapter 8 verse 11. "Because the sentence against an evil deed is not executed quickly, therefore the hearts of the sons of men among them are given fully to do evil."

'Squashing,' I thought.

"Yes," she said. "Squashing."

Loud, joyous music came from the arena where Wanda was about to speak. Then somber, meloncholy music.

I heard shouts of, "Magic Wanda, where is Magic Wanda? Magic Wanda, Magic Wanda, Magic Wanda."

"It's almost my time," she said

Wanda walked onto the stage. I was glad she wore very dark glasses onstage because the stage lights were intensely bright. The people stood and cheered. They chanted, Magic Wanda, Magic Wanda over and over.

She did not acknowledge the crowd with a nod or wave of hand. She looked out over the happy crowd of eighty something thousand people. She paused before stepping to the podium which floated with no visible support. She put her notes on the podium and stood and looked at the crowd as they cheered and clapped their hands and whistled, hooted, mewed and howled.

She turned her back to the crowd and she said to me, "They don't love me. They love Gus. This is why I like this."

Her words to me boomed through the speaker system and their cheers roared even louder.

She positioned herself at the floating podium and held out her hands, palms down and spoke.

She said, "Please, let's talk."

Silence.

"Let's talk about Ecclesiastes chapter 8 verse 11 that Gus dearly loved. It says; *Because the sentence against an evil deed is not executed quickly, therefore the hearts of the sons of men among them are given fully to do evil.*

Gus read this and it etched onto his heart. Gus begged God to tell him what is evil and what is the sentence.

God told Gus to read and see and what is evil and then He will tell him the sentence once seen.

Gus read and found that evil is violence and treachary.

And God told Gus, The sentence is ...."

Wanda paused and it seemed everyone there all at once said with intense energy, conviction and humor, "SQUASHING."

"Yes, yes Squashing," Wanda said. "Yes, yes Squashing."

She continued, "Biddle dee dee, ponky wonky, snaxie, dreen, fig blazoons, paunchy waters of dreadness. It is as it is. Evil must be squashed quickly and every single time."

Wanda paused then danced for a few minutes. High energy but sad music wqas played. Wanda whirled an twirled rhythmically like Twyla Tharpe. People stood and clapped and danced. Assorted and abstract shouts of joy and praise rose up.

I could hear, "Thank you God for Gus and Wanda."

She stopped her dance and raised her hands and said, "Seek God's love and share it. Seek God's love and share it. Seek God's love and share it. Remember to walk. I love you."

Then she walked off the stage.

The crowd was singing the words she left them with.

Wanda grabbed a microphone offstage and she sang to the people through the sound system.

It's in your heart
It's on your skin
Guard your mind
It's from within

THE SLIME SLIDES DOWN
Into the sun
Light dries it out
It's dusty fun

YOUR THOUGHTS ARE HOLY holy moly
Guard them like a rabid dog
Holy spirits come to help you
Protect them like a mama hog

It's in your heart
It's on your skin
Guard your mind
It's from within

SHE SANG THIS SONG so gentle and swaying rhythmic. She sang through it only once. Sometimes she warbled just sounds. There is a harmonic sound to her voice.

Chapter 17

Going to a Squashing With Wanda

WANDA'S WALKING ALONG a highway alone.
Lightly I whisper, "Satchmo."
She's singing and strumming simple guitar chords

TORMENT THEM WITH PLATYPUS venom
The torturers are tortured
No no I don't have pity for them
For they tortured children and women and men
No one dare feel mercy for them
Just torment n squash em
Torment n squash em
Torment n squash em oh man Amen
I'm over it I'm over it
Squash em Squash em Squash em
Yeah muh baby Yeah muh baby
Yeah Yeah Yeah

THEN SHE STARTED DANCING and jumping and whirling around. It felt so very good.

"Hey Sparky, you thought I didn't hear you Satchmo didn't you?

A glorious squashing is happening in the city two days walk away. Many from a cult of child abusing monsters are to be squashed and some of them will be injected with Duck Billed Platypus venom an hour before squashing because they are henious torturers. I love it!"

I said, 'I'm starting to see why and how you celebrate the good punishing the evil since most of our life experience we've seen and felt the torment of the good by the evil.'

"Yes Sparky, you've said it."

'Let's Harpo,' I said. 'I'll save my questions and comments. I just want to see and feel what you do.'

"Satchmo, well I guess," she said, pretending I'd hurt her feelings.

When we reach the Squashing Festival there will be a lot to see and do. I'm sure I can find some one to talk to. Since you prefer not to talk with me Mister high and mighty independent Sparky of Earth."

'You're toying with me,' I said. 'I just don't want to clutter your mind with my oohs and ahs and ughs.'

"Oh Sparky, little sweet, simple, primitive Sparky. Yes oh yes I'm toying with you. Harpo!" she said with bristle.

I said, 'Satchmo, come on Wanda, are we okay?'

"Oh sure. Harpo," she said.

'Well Harpo it is then,' I thought. 'She's just playing, I think.'

Is this stress I feel in her? I never imagined stress in Wanda's spirit. She's like wind, like water, like radiant energy flowing by nature by design. It must be fatigue or some tenser I'm not aware of.

"Satchmo," she said. "Satchmo damnit."

'Hi Sweetie,' I said.

"Your dang, blinkin, stinkie I'm a sweetie. I'm just here flopping and dying like a fish in the dirt. You better love me, stupid, because if you do then you love something good and if you really love something good, you become something good. You stupid, stupid, I speak of the universal you here, Sparky. Stupid."

'What's going on Wanda?'

"I'm tense Sparky."

'Are you smoking a pipe?'

"Yes, God told me to smoke a tobacco pipe. God told Gus to do many odd things like he told Elijah to stand naked by the road. One time God told Gus to do a one minute commercial spot where he repeated over and over – (A time will come when many will say that Squashing is not from God: Don't believe them.) Gus spoke this over some beautiful, sorrowful instrumental music that included a heart-soaring vocal chorus of sustained harmonized tones. I get emotional thinking of it. I listen to it still.

God has told me He will use my tobacco use to reveal to the spiritually blind their dark hearts so they will take them in for lighting."

We were nearing the Squashing Festival, seeing more and more walkers going to attend. The day was glorious. Wanda walked on. I could feel a lightness in her steps like she had resolved some burden in her heart.

'Wanda, Wanda.' I thought

"Sparky, Sparky, yes." she said.

People were gathering at the large open field that surrounds the Squashing Disk. The polished disk dazzles in the bright sun. Loud electronic rhythmic music plays. I can tell some people recognize Wanda, but they leave her alone because they are not idiots.

Wanda was handed a 5 by 7 card, a lovely pale green with a bright yellow daisy on the front. Also on the front in brown ink it read:

Welcome to a Squashing

Inside in brown ink was printed.

Freely they had the chance to be free from evil acting, but instead they chose to be squashed. Today's squashees are a married couple, Solvun and her husband Turrug. Crime: Physical and sexual abuse of children. Proof: Their own personal video recordings and official nanocam recordings procured by planetary officials once preponderant suspicioun had been purloined by enlightened observers. Have a great squashing day.

Please note: Due to the horrific nature of the suffering inflicted on the victims by the squashees, Duck Billed Platypus venom will be injected into the evil, one hour prior to actual squashing. If you don't wish to see the evil writhing in agony and hear them scream from the searing pain then turn away from the jumbo screen and turn up your earphone receivers and enjoy the tremendous music and as always, dancing is encouraged.

'Are you going to watch them suffer?' I asked.

"Oh yes" she said. "The suffering they gave their victims is as horrible as you've ever

heard of , long, drawn out over days, sometimes weeks. Makes you want to stab their eyes out with a screwdriver and tie them in the sun to dehydrate to death. Platypus venom for an hour would be mercy for their victims. The kind of evil they carried out, besides making me sick, just really," Wanda screamed almost cyring, "Pisses me off!"

'I'm with you Wanda.' I said.

She told me that for crime less horrific than this there is little fanfare. They just squash em, but for something as heinous as this there are some rituals.

One is they ask the condemned if they have anything to say, but the squashing team has sprayed a solution on their vocal cords that temporarily keeps them from speaking. Then the squashers ask them if they have anything to say and when they try to talk the crowd and the squashers scream, "We don't care. We only want to hear your victims speak, but they cannot." Then everyone sits quietly wihile the venom is injected. The vocal chord numbing agent wears off and they always cry out and moan and beg for death.

This is where we are. Solvun and Turrug are in a transparent dome, a few feet across and tall enough for them to stand in. They are bound to chairs while being injected. When the injection is complete then the squashers leave the dome and the condemned are unfettered remotely.

The venom courses through their bodies and their pain receptors fire as if they are being slowly burned alive. Their vocal chords come back to life. They scream, they writhe, squirm and moan. They jerk and spasm as if they lie on a hot skillet. A compound in the injection keeps them from going into shock and passing out.

Wanda tells me, "Most people think they want to see this, but they really don't. The crowd usually starts to chant, squash em, squash em. But the full hour must be carried out. Most turn up their headphones after a time, look away and dance."

This is just how it happened. Most looked away, but not Wanda. She watched and listened to her music on low volume and danced as if in a trance. It feels great.

THE TRAIL PLANET WITH HAMMOCKS

Wanda raised her hands and in a loud voice said, "Thank You God for the future victims that you have made free and well today."

Wanda sang, "Leave well alone and seek the Father

Leave well alone and find His love

Leave well alone and know the only good goal is to seek His Love"

Chapter 18

Remembering

There are four or five wrens having a squabble near my tent, speaking in that way that humans can't mimic.

Is man the freak of this Earth just to experience terror and despair? Aren't we as worthy as a toad to live without anxiety and just live by God-given impulse? Maybe we share nothing with the animals that know no shame and dread.

Maybe this is a prayer. I don't want to worry anymore. Worry creates nothing. Maybe there is no way not to worry.

The cries and moans of the punished are fresh in my mind as I plod through the bleariness of waking this morning. I did not hear the hideous couple's screams and pleas as we watched them writhe under the effects of the venom. Their sounds of agony only reminded me of the pain and terror of their victims. I did not get squeamish. I wanted to hurt them more.

There are times I want to disappear, feel nothing, sense nothing, be nothing. I can fall asleep in that state but moments after I wake I'm entangled again in things I have no hint of control over, which is nearly everything. This is why Jesus told us not to worry. So I try.

The past few weeks Wanda has watched, ney, obsessed over, absorbed, incorporated into her soul a video presentation about the Ocean Moon. I lounge here at my camp in my lounging chair drinking coffee alone with no complimentary tobacco smoke. What the hell. I don't care. My addicted brain is like an asshole, persistent demon calling me a punk, sissy afraid of death and COPD. Saying you love tobacco and what you have to do is what you like. I lie back and watch the Ocean Moon video Wanda imprinted on my brain with closed eyes.

Blues, greens, purples, pinks the video just shows the water. Then some scrubby trees around inland water laden with birds blue, green, yellow and pink singing, squawking, tweeting, flying in flying out and around, some with beaks full of fish or insects. Pan to hundreds of butterflies, some colored exactly like rainbows, others bright yellow, green, blue, purple, red, orange. The Ocean Moon may be nearest a physical paradise as can be.

Small, medium and large boats all over, oddly all with white hulls.

Close-ups of jumping fish in slow motion, some irradescent blue green like Mahi Mahi, Dolphin Fish.

Wanda spent a lot of time watching again and again a part of the Ocean Moon video about the Transparent Domed Cruise Ships that sail to the frigid regions and the very hot regions of the moon. These are so cool. These ships have a glorious sparkling dome under which is climate controlled. The video shows scenes of the life rich cold oceans of the moon. I see whales like crazy, seals, walri, penguins, fish like wowzie. Islands busy with geothermal zones. I see people walking in summer clothes in these steamy zones. They risk sudden death or hideous burns from random expulsions. Wanda has explained to me that most Trail Planetons consider a life of fear with no freedom is much more to feared than death while enjoying.

Snow falls softly.

A poem popped in so I grab my notebook to capture it.

CAN MY HEART DWELL on Jesus and I still do my work
    Jesus tells me only He is life
    I believe Him
    There is nowhere else to go
    The branch withers
    There is no peace
    No life apart from Jesus
    I can do my work and my heart dwell on Jesus.

IT SEEMS WANDA HAS few human interactions, much like myself. I have difficulty bearing human melodrama. Not because I'm some logic master or scientist, I'm no freakin scientist. It just all seems so pointless. No one knows how they came to be or really where they're going. So strange. I know I'm without a clue. A condition shared by all. I wonder what Wanda is doing. How did Gus do it? Turn a race from stupid to not stupid. Squash enough evil to tip the balance. Could I, Sparky, with my knowledge of the Trail Planet stem the tide of dull insanity of Earth humans? I laugh and laugh very loud at this thought like a mad maniac I laugh and laugh. A group of helmeted eight to twelve year olds ride by on bicycles, look my way and speed off chattering about me.

Make it profitable to benefit even the dullest of Earth humans. I love Sam Walton. He's nearly an example of this. He made maple syrup affordable for the very poor and he profited himself and his progeny in the process.

What am I talking about? Most times I feel I'm barely surviving. Maybe I'll start the billboard program I've dreamed of. Who knows?

BITTERNESS AND FEAR Attract Dark Spirits
    Faith and Love the opposite

THAT COULD BE MY FIRST.

Chapter 19

M oon Waves

MOST OF TODAY I'VE been on the beach. A little swim, a little sun, a little beer, six or seven nicotine lozenges. I read a few chapters of the Franzine Turnbee novel, 'What the Hell Stupid' which I am loving and I read some Bible. I read the chapters in Romans that tell about righteousness through faith. Thank God for that, literally.

Wanda has not made contact with me for three or four days. I've spent some time with Fran pleasantly but I haven't seen the Trail Planet for too long. The free-moving, eccentric people with their crazy long braided hair or shaved tattooed heads, the music, the free-roaming children, the rivers, streams, mountains, oceans and glorious Creator-praising plants and animals. I am longing for the trails and missing my children. They are dancing light.

Lying in my hammock my eyes are want to stay closed. My mind glides to the Trail Planet searching for Wanda.

"Hello Sparky," I hear Wanda say in her teasing way.

'Wanda, where oh where have you been? I'm drying up like a dead desert toad here in the Earth. I see and feel we are kayaking on a cool, gentle river. Thank God you're back. I thought we'd been disconnected.'

"No, I've just been busy. I've been practicing guitar and working up my songs; Because, because; Are you ready? Listen, I've been hired to play and sing one night a week at a resort on the Ocean Moon."

'Hooray for you!' I thought. 'So I too will see and feel the Ocean Moon with you.'

"Yes, yes, yes." she said.

I see and feel her toned, tanned arms paddling left and right down the gentle, cool, green river. No pain in her back and shoulders. Sweat glistens on her hands. She lays the paddle across her lap and stretches back then wipes the sweat from beneath her breasts covered only by a sheer lavender top.

"Sparky, I'm learning to see in Spirit. In doing this I'm realizing something peculiar, something I find hard to believe, but I believe it. That is that the entire physical universe was created for us to learn to overlook or look through as if it isn't there and see the Spirit of Christ that is more marvelous than the creation."

'Like seeing things that are not as if they are,' I thought.

"More like seeing things that are as if they are."

'Or seeing things that are as if they are not.'

"More like there is one thing real, the Spirit of Christ. There is nothing else. And it's like all the things we've said. Take great care in what you say about yourself and others in audible words or thoughts. In Proverbs 13 it says 'From the fruit of a man's mouth he enjoys good' It's really important what we speak. Darkness is the accuser, the depresser, the destroyer. What we speak and think will align us with darkness or light."

'I'm excited for you Wanda and for me because we get to see the Ocean Moon. When do we go?'

"Very soon."

She stopped the kayak on a bright white sandbar. She pulled a light towel from her bag and spread it on the soft, fine, warm sand. She lay on the towel. Her eyes closed we listen to birds and gentle wind.

Chapter 20

To the Moon

I FIND MYSELF IN WANDA'S existence again. This time she is strapped into a comfortable airline seat in an aircraft like a space shuttle. The stewardesses are doing a final check to be sure everyone is securely strapped in. All the stewaredesses then strapped into their seats. One radioed the captain to say the passengers and flight crew are prepared for take off.

The Captain announced, "All passengers and crew remain in your take off posture. Taking off momentarily."

I don't hear any roaring engines, then, oh Mama I feel Wanda squished hard into her seat. Her stomach goes queasy with the G's.

Wanda is singing

.

I got love in my bones I got love bones
I got holes in my shoes I got holy shoes
My heart is like a flying bird
I fly along on holy words
I sing to you cause I'm in love
With all of God's creation

SOMETIMES I CRY AND taste the tears
I want to cry tears for you

I know where you want to go to
I will see you there
Very near Him

AS WE APPROACHED THE Ocean Moon we were treated to video images of our approach. The blue-green water shimmered on the screen.

Wanda said, "I'm getting excited Sparky. This is going to be so great. The animals, the people, you're going to love it. We have to go eat fish."

We made our way through the terminal. The terminal is like a gallery with glorious, mostly abstract paintings. Every fifty yards or so musicians played. Wanda stopped to listen and dance. She put polkas in many of their instrument cases. The music of most was joyful and full of faith and beauty. Some music was dramatic, emotive and rich. It stirred Wanda's insides and made her heart warm and calm. I purposed in this moment to seek out the rich and textured beauty of human expression and immerse myself in it when I wake and my consciousness is back in the Earth. No more self-assigned exile from the life God allows and even wills for me if I will only step out of the dreary lies of evil. Coming out of the dank cellar shelter starting now. Wanda has only a backpack and her guitar in it's beautifully decorated case. She walks a brisk pace to reach a meal of fresh Ocean Moon fish.

Chapter 21

Chain Reaction of Deterioration of Brain Tissue

I'M IN A BUBBLE OF thought. I feel like I'm only thought. I know there are many things but they are only what I think of them.

You've got a short time
To go a long way
but you are already there
You are already there

THE LYRICS OF THIS song Wanda says made her finally an unabashed believer in Gus Way and Gus Way is only a pointer to the ultimate.

In the beginning was the Word and the Word was with God and the Word was God.

My brain is down to the size of a walnut now. I can barely put two words together.The Brain Nugget has caused a chain reaction of deterioration of my brain tissue.

It's a love thing.

Chapter 22

N ot So Far Away

IT TURNS OUT MY BRAIN has not deteriorated. It just felt that way. I have a great deal of difficulty living here as a human on the Earth. It seems many have this difficulty. There's much I don't care for here. Seeing the Trail Planet cheers me though. Although I wondered sometimes if Wanda was bored with the peace and harmony of her world with very little to fear and very little deprivation. Wanda set me straight on that question though.

Chapter 23

You Idiot

"Of course, you idiot, I hate it here. It's sooo boring not fearing for my life and my autonomy. I don't fear that I will be forced into something I don't want to do. I don't fear that my children will be in desperate want of basic things. I don't fear that I will be destitute and rejected. I hate it. I see evil squashed as soon as possible. Oh yes I hate it. I see human effort for enhancement of the human experience. I hate it. I'm bored. Shut up you dense as mud victim of Earth. What the fractal is wrong with you?"

She had never cursed at me before. Of course she was right. I am an Earth Human, therefore something of an idiot. Lord Jesus help me. And I'm so grateful that He does. I'm a blithering dead dolt without Him.

Chapter 24

On Ocean Moon Beach

"I never get tired of the beach." Wanda said.

'Nor I,' I said.

We're walking an expansive beach. Miles and miles of Wanda alone. Forever surf

Rolling in, small white caps further out. The sand white like Pensacola beach but with sparkling highlights of pink and turquoise. My heart and Wanda's race at the beauty of the blue-green, turquoise and cobalt blue wildly outlined to infinity with the gorgeous sand. The beach, sometimes ten meters, sometimes hundreds wide and where the bare sand ends, plants similar to those in parts of California, sage-like but many varieties. The fragrance of the sage and rosemary and the salt ocean put the mind in the heaven.

Wanda walks and walks, her backpack weighs about thirty pounds. I love being in her body. Muscled like a fit tennis player. Stamina like a triathlete. No pain in legs or back. She has energy to spare.

Wanda said, "Those structures ahead that look like wide-based obelisks and some a bit like Easter Island heads contain kayaks and fishing gear and can be used for shelter. They have water, coffee, drinks and simple foods available there in gratuity. It's a great job they have who make the rounds supplying these beach supply shelters. Good polkas I hear.

Turns out a truck was stopped on the other side of the maybe two thousand square foot cabin tent shaped we were approaching. It has fat wheels for the sand. The shelter was of a sturdy material that was very thin. Wanda said the material does not denature at all and should last a thousand years or more.

Inside there are kayaks against the wall, fishing gear and food and drink. There's a box to contribute polkas. Wanda put her thumb into a reader next to the contribution box and she's quickly id'ed. She keys in a polka amount of a hundred. I don't know if this is a lot.

"Sort of, for me," Wanda says.

We hear a man singing. He is stocking the food dispensers.

"Hello," he says to Wanda.

"Greetings," she says.

Being a man I know he finds Wanda attractive. Not surprising.

I am Torgin, Ocean Moon beach shelter supplier and you are?"

"Wanda, songwriter and Gus speaker. What a great job you have. Do you love it?"

"Oh yes, can't beat the working conditions making rounds in near paradise."

He was of course fitter than a fiddle and clearly virile. It showed but there was no embarrassment.

Wanda said, "I am a brain nugget host and I'm showing my Earth friend Sparky the Ocean moon."

"Hello Sparky. You are a blessed human. It must be a joy seeing through Wanda's eyes and feeling her being."

I thought, 'Tell him it is indeed. The spirit of Earth is generally dark. It hurts me to exist in the Trail Planet way then return, but yes I am blessed.'

Wanda told him.

They spoke a little longer and exchanged phone numbers.

Wanda said, "Sparky and I are off to explore Torgin. I will contact you while I still have time on the moon."

Torgin said, "Would you mind telling me something from Gus' writings before you go?"

Wanda said, "God has supplied all the energy, provision and faith needed for humans, only dark human spirits are the makers of deprivation. Believe, trust, live in freedom. Turn to darkness and be rightly squashed. Take time to pray."

Torbin said, "Thanks. The next shelter is two miles away. Be aware of the tides. Great meeting you."

He was pleasant, joyful, enthusiastic. He watched Wanda walk away for many for a long time. She glanced back to see.

Wanda, I and the elements now. Birds of all sorts, most looked like they had an Earth relative. One bird looked like a Great Blue Heron searching in pools on the beach. Mostly white with some blue and pink patterns on his back and with black feathers on his head that looked like dreads about eight inches long.

About thirty minutes Wanda did not speak and I did not think into her consciousness. Wind, blue sky, jeweled water, bird sounds, fish feeding, some jumping, some gliding like flying fish, dolphin breathing and occasional people, they glistened, they did not speak.

Wanda gathered some exquisite shells into her pocket. One like a scalloop shell two inches across, intact but with a hole in it. She pulled a leather boot lace from her other pocket and made a necklace of it. It dazzled in her hand orange and purple. This is a woman so much to my liking.

She walked into the water. It was delicious. Her strong legs, steady in the nearshore turbulence .

'I love you,' I thought.

"I love you Sparky," she said.

She looked further up the beach and saw a solid floatie. She walked to retrieve it. We lie on the on her back and and paddled out fifty yards. She wore most efficient sunglasses lying there up and down with the ocean. Fish jumped over sometimes and dolphin porpoised nearby.

"You can write songs Sparky in your time on Earth. Glorify what should be and call what is ugly and useless ugly and useless. I'm feeling it Sparky, I feel all the energy and creative force of God and God's energy going into my belly. It's driving me mad. Elijah must have felt this sometimes. I think all humans that know their place with God feel this sometimes. Grace, love, provision for all is what I pray. Wisdom to know our position in God. There is a conduit open that supplies us energy and illumination when we know our position.

God made everything Sparky. The ocean we're lying on. The space I'm staring into. Sun, stars, moon, magma. Good comes when we cease struggling. Our main goal is to realize our position with God. We are utterly dependent on God's provision. God controls so more than we can comprehend. Imagine your parents control 40 trillion dollars. Pray Sparky. God can do anything. Always know that God knows best. I desire to know what God says is evil and to resist, flee and expose it.

Sometimes I just want to stop and say, God you're it, because I know that no human, other than Jesus Christ has any understanding of the state we are in. We remain at all times dependent on God's love and mercy.

I've been learning what God says is evil. The biggest thing is worshipping anything other than the true Creator God of Love."

I said, 'That's so true. God's word is full of direction to worship no other. It makes clear sense. If we worship the True Creator God of Love and love Him then we become more like Him in desire, and the act of worshipping Him and standing in our position of dependence protects us from the multitude of deceivers. Faith and love are not passive and impotent, but vital and disarming.'

Wanda said, "We don't squash for idolatry but the squashed are rarely lovers of the True Creator God of Love."

We both went quiet. After a few minutes we felt the warm air again and the cool water. We felt the ocean surface massauge the mat up and down. Wanda stroked back to the beach.

Wanda began the walk back along the surfline to where the beach walk began.

A few minutes walking then Wanda said, "I want to tell you a story. Do you want to hear it?"

'Yes.'

"When I was living in mountain places and painting. Someone started mailing me their paintings, writings and instrumental musis recordings.

They did not identify themselves. I didn't know if it was a man or woman. All I knew of them was the creative pieces they shared. It was a little creepy. At first I thought it was just a friend and they would soon let me know it was from them if they saw it was concerning me a little.

Over 2 years I got 23 paintings and drawings, 47 literary pieces of different types, some poems, some sayings, some short fiction, and 13 instrumental recordings.

After a few months I was no longer concerned about being stalked since nothing scary had occurred and the creative pieces were very appealling to me and were not romantic or pleading. I began looking forward to receiving the next thing.

In the little cottage I was living in I had many of the visual art pieces displayed. I listened to the music I received much of the time when I was reading, writing, painting, exercising or meditating.

The literary pieces and drawings I made into a book. I sold the book under the psuedonym Pamalena. Many of these books were sold and I received a substantial number of polkas. The book became a little famous.

When the book became well known I stopped receiving new mystery pieces of art. For many months nothing came. Then I received a photograph sent as a postcard. The image on the photo was of an irredescent blue, yellow and green fly on a white daisy. Written on the back was this.

'What you know of me is in the thing I created. This is exactly what we know of God when we observe anything in the universe. I love you. If you want to send me polkas for my contribution to the book, send to Pine Cone at the following address.'

I sent a polka transfer for half what I received for the book and a note of thanks and admiration.

Chapter 25

B ack to Earth

WAKING IN MY TENT ON Earth I am sweating like Rosie Oprah Whoopi Joy, you know, the comedian, on a diet near a cheesecake. He is so funny. I'd been awake 23 hours before I had collapsed in my tent. I figured out that I'm not capable of doing the eat as little as you can stand diet, so I'm doing the run yourself into the ground diet. In my case the walk youself into the ground diet. I've been walking hours a day.

There are two things I'm sure of. God is God and we know nothing unless God lets us know.

During this time of movement til exhaustion I'm being delivered from addictions and near addictions. Wanda read to me the chapter in Gus Book. The book of assorted prayers.

This one stuck in my brain and has helped so much in my struggles.

"God please deliver me from addictions"

While trying to not be addicted, sometimes I sit, stand or lie and stare. This catatonia prompts my misfiring brain to pray.

"God please help me learn to live with my un-addicted brain. Oh Father it feels funny. Please help."

In this stage my brain feels funny my thoughts are not sunny. Maybe it is all life and death, life or death.

Trying to clear addiction, it's all I can think about. At least it occupies 90% of my thought time.

My new addiction is my time in Wanda on the Trail Planet or its' moon and movement. I still appreciate my Earth human existence. I just want it to be better.

Back in Wanda again, she is filling a beautiful pipe with Trail Planet tobacco. She is sitting on the beach lightly puffing and re-lighting. Watching the water, at least 30 minutes, she does not speak and I don't think into her head. It is wonderful. I determined to find the tobacco pipe my Mother had given me a few years before she died. My Mom had a full time cigarette addiction. She was in favor of my addiction switch to the tobacco pipe.

Wanda siad, "Baby steps Sparky, for humans it's baby steps. You know why? Because Jesus said to see His kingdom you must see as children. So once we understand the highest state we can reach as humans is that of an under 8 year old child. Completely helpless if left on our own. Then we know baby steps is what we can do. I can see this amazing ocean, the birds, the fish, the shells, the dolphin. I see the starlight light. I feel the starlight heat flow that makes the wind blow. I did not make one particle or wave of any of it, of my toenail, the driftwood, the salt or the sand. I am an utterly dependent baby. Knowing my place has sucked the dread and anxiety from me. I am loved of God."

It seems like about 4:00 in the afternoon. Wanda has stashed her pipe and is walking. Her walking feels so good to me. She's wearing a backpack.

"I'm camping tonight Sparky. I've seen beautiful images taken of the Ocean Moon night sky. When the Ocean Moon rotates away from the suns it's like being inside a shimmering sphere. The stars glitter with color. Some a steady color, some phasing through hues."

I thought, 'Ooh la la.'

"Ooh la la indeed," she said.

Wanda walks about an hour then stops where the dunes past the beach are higher and stretch forever inland.

"This is a good place to stop. I know you love a fire Sparky, so do I, especially a driftwood fire on a beach on the most beautiful ocean I've ever heard of."

There's lots of great driftwood nearby. A group of 3 islands is within view they appear forested.

She drops her pack and wanders gathering wood. In a few minutes she has enough for the night. The pieces are gorgeous, unique in color and shape.

There is a hammock nearby. Wanda needs a break and nestles into the hammock.

"Sparky, Sparky, Sparky," she said.

'Wanda, Wanda, Wanda,' I thought.

We repeated this a few times.

She said, "There is so little to discuss. We know so little truly."

I said, 'We're becoming like a long-married couple. We mull our existence in each other's presence.'

"It's beautiful isn't it?"

'It is in many ways.'

I feel her breathing going calm and steady and her perfect body relaxing into the hammock. The daylight is dimming as the Trail Planet begins to block the suns. Being in this warm, anxiety-free body relaxes me. It is profound. My more aged body's aches and pains are muted by the feel of her vigor. I'm in a meditative bliss. Wanda must be dreaming. I feel her twitch. She moans and sighs. I feel waves of tingles. I wish I could see the setting of her mind's experience.

Chapter 26

T he Driftwood Fire

WANDA CROUCHED NEAR the shallow bowl of sand she made that had some wood in its center. She pulled 3 tape strips off a ball the size of a grape, then placed it in the arranged wood.

"Three minutes 'til ignition," she said.

She mounded up some sand about 15 feet from the fire bowl. She pulled a pale blue, thin, soft cloth, the size of a large beach towel from her pack and spread it on the side of the mound facing the fire. The fire starter grape begins ignition, first with a little smoke, then accelerates to a grapefruit sized flame ball that makes a wooshing sound. Wanda pressed here and there to adjust her chaise lounge of sand, then settled her wondrous frame upon it.

She looked over the fire at the ocean horizon. The light is early evening perfect.

We both love where we are on the beach, on the Ocean Moon of The Trail Planet With Hammocks. Wanda doesn't speak and I don't think into her mind. The Brain Nugget in her brain has been enhanced and the enhancement sent to my Brain Nugget. The enhancement allows either of us to just think Harpo or Satchmo to close and open the communication link. We have both wished at times that I could hear her thoughts. We had discussed the pros and cons of that. I already think in a strange manner, because, I'm doing something that humans don't do, and that is, form cognitive language in my thoughts while my brain is asleep. Just one of the wonders of the nugget. The greatest is my experience as if I my brain is inside her brain experiencing the universe that she sees, feeling the heat or cold on her skin, the blinking of her eyes, her vitality and fatigue, her internal anxiety and emotion, and the near constant sense of harmony and faith that she feels. She is a wonderful, joyous, searching child in the universe of God The Creator. I am so blessed to have this experience. She loves Gus because he is up to now God's most gifted pointer to Jesus. She love Jesus because He is Jesus. She is now the most gifted pointer to Jesus. Every good gift is from The Creator. It's not like we are looking through the galaxy, but that we are blanketed by it.

The fire is well established and just the right size. Wanda stares at the starlight and absorbs it, then focuses on the shimmering ocean horizon.

"Satellite," she said.

She pointed to an object moving steadily through the stars.

'Are you sure it's not a UFO ?'

"Not likely, we don't trust alien visitors and their UFO's. We are prepared for them. I read about the last one that came to the Trail Planet surface. These space aliens were clearly very stupid. This case was the motivation for establishing the Space Alien Repellent shield around the Trail Planet and the Ocean Moon. These idiots from a planet they call Zirconium, yeah I know. They tried to abduct someone. Every Trail Planet citizen has an anti-abduction device that signals a response team and emits a strong electrical current and a powerful magnetic field that stuns the idiot and you can run away.

They were subdued and detained. The Zirconiumians were interviewed by a select brain-scientist panel and were determined to be hostile and dangerous. They were allowed to board their craft and told to leave and never return. When they reached a safe elevation they were vaporized.

There is now a defense shield around the planet and the Ocean Moon. An unknown craft cannot approach closely without authorization. Sometimes in a clear sky like this you will see one approach the shield then change course and retreat abruptly. It's kind of funny.

Most of the visitors we've had have been evil, dominance and treasure seeking. Most had to be vaporized."

We see meteorites, maybe 5 to 10 a minute. One struck the water 50 meters out a steam plume appeared for a few seconds. One hit the sand twenty feet from us sounding VAP when it struck. Wanda walked over and marked the spot with a stick. She settled back down, then one hit her in her left calf. It was tiny. It stung and burned like a wasp sting.

She cried out, "Shite that hurt. This has happened to me before. The meteorite is so hot that it's sterile so I don't have to worry much about infection."

She took a small dropper bottle from her pocket and put one drop on the wound. The pain went away on contact.

A really bright one appeared exactly where she was looking.

"Did you hear it Sparky? Did you hear it vaporize? Sheeeyoop! That was so cool, sheeeyoop. I've never heard one vaporize before. Have you?"'No, I haven't. That was incredible. I don't remember how fast meteorites are travelling in the atmosphere.'

"It differs depending on the mass of the planet or moon and the angle into the atmosphere and all that. I think I read 10 to 50 thousand miles per hour. It was beautiful to see and sounded musical and powerful."

She lay back in her sand sculpture chaise and stared into the universe. I harpoed.

What do I see? I truly don't know. I pray. It's what I know to do. My mind holds to no patterns. I am lost in the depths of God's creaion. I am a non-being, but I must be some sort of being. I do sense a self. Muons and galaxies pass through me. I wait for my artist. I want to be still and mute before I am loud. I want to be loud with words that feed the Spirit of love and wisdom. Feeding, nurturing, welcoming, promoting, honoring,facilitating the Spirit of love, beauty, wisdom is the job for me. I give up but I continue. I am no match for the cosmos.

Chapter 27

T initus

DISCONNECTED FROM WANDA, at my campsite, in my hammock I focus on my tinitus. I haven't always had tinitus, but I don't remember not having it. It sounds like a chorus of frogs and insects. This passes as entertainment for me because I've recently realized I have little interest in anything. My body feels like a layover on a journey. It doesn't feel like somewhere. Even if I could really live in this body and mind on the Trail Planet, I would love the greater freedom and joy for a while, but, I believe I would arrive again at this station, between worlds, maintaining on hope of a real world worth the trouble.

I've learned a few tricks having survived past 50 years. When I feel this empty I've learned to be a plant. I sit. I still exist, still alive, but I make no moves because decisions made from the premise that everything is futile often lead to a quagmire.

Adjusting my sleep mask I sense my mass repelled by the fabric of the hammock. If my hammock were to cease to exist the gravity of the mass of Earth would pull me to the ground with a thud. I wonder how far you have to go from the Earth you have to go to be free from the Earth's gravity. I'll look it up sometime. I mean far enough so you wouldn't get stuck in orbit.

Breath continues. I dwell on it. Christ is moving, heart flexing, releasing. Ah yes I control my existence. My face is expressionless but my soul laughs with abandon.

Chapter 28

G us: Art Salesman

BACK IN WANDA AGAIN.

She says, "Sparky, I want to tell you more about Gus."

'Please,' I reply.

"Gus worked. It took him a long time to be convinced he was an artist touched by the Creator, given words, images and music to communicate with humans. Once Gus fully understood that the Creator wished to use him like a pencil, pen or brush to market and advertise to His beloved free-will humans, then he was freed to become an art salesman, a marketer of the pieces he was entrusted with. He became obsessed with the best art salesman of all time and he represented only his own literature, image and music. He understood that if you don't have an agent, marketing department or advocate, then you are your agent, marketing department and advocate. He said in his autobiography that he grew to love marketing, marketing the truth, marketing the Creator's wishes. One of his favorite directives from the Bible is Micah 6:8,'Do justice, love kindness, walk humbly with your Creator'. Gus loved the phrases that were so clear, so concise concerning what is pleasing to the Creator.

There was a long pause. I'd been enraptured with her monologue. I appreciate what a gift Wanda has to so love Gus and the Creator and be obsessed with Gus art.

"Sparky, in 3 weeks I leave the Ocean Moon. I've decided to live somewhere for a time. I mean live in a home with a porch and a studio. I'm going to decorate it with Gus art and my own."

I thought, "I feel something I have felt very little of in you Wanda, and that is anxiety, a sort of nervous energy. Are you okay?"

She laughed and said, "Yes, yes I'm okay. I'm fearful of nothing in particular. The solid ground of my mind is crumbled somewhat. Like Creator is pushing me somewhere and like a timid child I'm resisting. As beautiful as the Trail Planet is, it's still a mystery to exist and be aware of being. I believe there is something real beyond this and I long for it."

Chapter 29

What Mass in the Universe is This

OKAY, NOW I'M 60 YEARS old. I wonder what is really worth it? Love is what I keep hearing. That's what's worth it. That's what's worth promoting.

Am I having this Wanda, Gus experience so I can market Gus revelation of the Creator? Do justice, love kindness, walk humbly with your Creator? Love, kindness, love, love really? Only love makes the Earth anything worth it. Without love the Earth should be destroyed.

I remember a Gus poem Wanda shared with me. She told me Gus wrote this a few months before he finally was convinced by the Creator that he should promote love and justice and humility on the Trail Planet. It's queer that I remember it, because I don't remember things well. That's one reason I'm not a comedian, a musician or an actor. Gus was nearing his moment of clarity. The breaking through the cloud of lying voices to finally reach the point of focus, to understand his purpose, to see at last, at least in his waning years that he was meant to be a promoter of the love and life-affirming way.

YOUR MASS BY GUS
There is precious little mass in the universe
A tear in the ocean
The most important mass is the mass of your physical body

Your mass is the champion
Is the revolutionary soldier
Yours is the mass that may change the perception of human existance
Because the Creator loves you

WHY DOES IT SEEM SO hopeless? I'm too old to wonder these things, but I don't care, I'm 60 years old, I have 20 or 30 more years, maybe more, maybe less to do something. I'm going to be set free from diversion and deception. I'm going to write about love and know that it is as useless, futile and pointless as anything else. I do it for fun. I do it for love.

My brain, my perception, my bluebird song, it's all for you. We are stranded here all together 'til death, and we may go on together beyond death.

Another Gus poem plays in my mind.
I need to be in the quiet.

I NEED TO BE IN THE Quiet by Gus
　　I need to be in the quiet
　　No voices
　　No music
　　Because The Holy Spirit speaks softly
　　I need blue sky, clouds, stars, dirt, green plants
　　I need every sub-atomic particle
　　I need every energy of the universe
　　To hear the sound of The Holy Spirit
　　To speak of love

THE MIRAGE IS FORMING and compelling me forward. I will clank and rattle to contrast love and darkness, love and dissipation and destruction.

God's fascination for life, love, energy, rhythm and pattern is astounding. Emotion, love, heartache, joy, faith, kindness, humility all boundless miracles. I want to love God's passions and obsessions. I want to spend my human body in their illumination. Love and faith are the guide. I pray my children and all my loves have peace and strength from God in their lives.

Chapeter 30
In a Tree

THE LAST COUPLE NIGHTS when I sleep I haven't found myself in Wanda.

Lounging in Fran's cabin, we are watching a new Investigation Channel story about a young woman who had been brutalized by a couple, man and woman. She'd been held captive, chained in a cellar until they chose to go see her, free her and toy with her with physical and emotional torture and debase her sexually.

I said to Fran, "Squashing after platypus venom injection is appropriate here."

She said, "Oh yeah and maybe some strategic flesh burning."

We cuddle, snuggle, nuzzle and light up each others senses in joy. I think we are in love.